OFF THE ICE

NEW YORK TIMES BESTSELLING AUTHOR

L.P. DOVER

Off The Ice

Edited by Kiezha Ferrell at Librum Artis—https://librumartis.com/

Cover Design—Letitia Hasser at RBA Designs

Interior Formatting & Design—T.E. Black Designs; www.teblackdesigns.com

A NOTE FROM THE AUTHOR

This book is dedicated to all my Breakaway lovers out there. The series was a joy to write, and I'm going to miss it terribly. Especially Maddox and Justin—they were my favorites to write. Thank you for sticking with my hockey men, and showing them your love.

THANK YOU FOR YOUR SUPPORT!

CHAPTER ONE

JUSTIN

THERE WERE ONLY THIRTY SECONDS left on the clock, the score one to one. All eyes were on me and Maddox. It reminded me of those snowy days back in Minnesota when Maddox and I played against the neighborhood boys on my backyard's iced-over pond. That was the beginning of our hockey dream. This was his last game before retirement, and I had to make sure he went out a winner. Everyone was counting on me.

My heart pounded relentlessly in my chest, but everything around me moved in slow motion. Maddox had the puck, but Brock Hansen, Pittsburgh's cunt of a forward, charged up behind him.

"*Look out*!" I shouted.

Maddox deviated and passed me the puck just as Brock lunged toward him, missing him by a hair and crashing into the wall. "Ha-ha cocksucker," Maddox chuckled.

The puck was mine. I didn't have time to think. There were only fifteen seconds left, and now it was all up to me. We'd won our fair share of games this season, but we'd also lost some—and those losses were mostly ones *I'd* screwed up. I never should have agreed to be the bachelor on *Rich and Single.* Ever since I signed that contract, my life had been nothing but a huge clusterfuck. Not anymore.

The Stanley Cup would belong to the Charlotte Strikers once again.

I can do this. Tonight would be the beginning of my freedom ... in more ways than one.

"Come on, Davis! Let's win this!" Coach Kellan roared. The crowd around the arena jumped to their feet as I raced toward the goal, their cheers and chants ringing in my ear. Only five seconds left. Four. Three...

I took one last breath and hit the puck, holding the air in my lungs as I watched it sail across the ice. It was almost like an out-of-body experience. The ending buzzer echoed all around us, but not before the puck found its home.

"The Strikers win the Stanley Cup again!" Hearing those words brought me back.

Maddox threw his arms around me, just as my other teammates lifted me in the air. I could only describe it as the best feeling in the world. I belonged on the ice. Tossing off my helmet, I waved at our fans with the biggest grin on my face. This was what I wanted to be known for being, a hockey player ... not a reality show star.

Cameras flashed all around us as the guys set me down in front of Kellan, our coach. Up until this last season he had been one of us–and he was still the backbone of our team.

"Good job, guys. You've made me proud tonight." More cameras flashed. "Now let's get out of here and celebrate."

The guys hooted and hollered as we skated off the ice behind Kellan, right toward the reporters. Maddox slapped his hands on my shoulders, snickering low. "Looks like they want an interview with the star of the night. And heads up, your girl's right behind them, trying to get through."

The thought of pretending with Miranda another second made me so goddamn sick. I pitied any man who got wrangled into her mess. What made it worse was that I'd lost a year of my life and a lot of my sanity, all because of a stupid contract.

The second I stepped off the ice, reporters shouted my name, thrusting their microphones in my face. "How does it feel to win the Stanley Cup again?" one of them asked.

I saw Miranda trying to break through the crowd. She was in for a rude awakening. "Amazing," I answered quickly, trying my best to get down the line. Just a few more steps and I'd be in the locker room, away from her.

Only two more reporters left to get through. Of course, one of them asked the million-dollar question. "So, Justin, tell us how our famous bachelor and his fiancée are going to celebrate this victory?" The young reporter smiled for the camera, but it slowly faded when he got a look at my face. *The famous bachelor.* Not the star center forward for the Charlotte Strikers—just the famous bachelor. What a fucking joke. I couldn't blame it on him though; I did it to myself.

Chuckling, I glanced down at his name badge, relieved that my punishment was over. "Oh, Allen, funny you should mention that. As of right now, my fiancée and I are no more. I'm officially free. I plan on celebrating this victory with my team." I looked up at the ceiling, clasping my hands together in praise. "Thank God."

Gasps of surprise erupted from the line of reporters, followed by bursts of laughter from my teammates. "What?" Miranda screamed. She'd come into view, hands on her hips with that bitchy snarl on her face. "You can't be serious."

All cameras turned her way and then back to me. A smug

smile spread across my face. "Oh, I am." Then I turned my back on her and walked away.

FOR THE FIRST TIME IN a year, I could breathe. Was it a mistake to do what I did on national TV? Probably. There was nothing I could do about it now. What was done, was done. Miranda needed to be taken down a notch or twelve. It was a good thing I was leaving town for a while. All I had to do was get through the after party and make my flight to Wyoming tomorrow morning.

When I pulled up at Sammy's Pub, there was already a line of reporters. I was pretty sure they wanted more than pictures from me after the show I'd put on at the stadium. So far, Miranda was nowhere to be seen, but that wouldn't last long.

Dallas, the Strikers' goalie and my brother-in-law, parked right beside me, shaking his head. My sister waddled over to my car. In about eight weeks, I was going to be an uncle. Hands on her hips, it was obvious she didn't agree with what I'd done.

"I know what you're going to say," I said, getting out of my car. The air was thick with humidity like it always was in the south during summer. "But you, of all people, know how bad I wanted to put Miranda in her place."

Callie sighed, and her face softened. We both had the same blonde hair and green eyes like our mother, but she had inherited our mother's stubborn streak. Dallas gave me a thumbs-up and winked before draping his arm around her shoulders. Callie smacked him on the stomach. "Don't think for one second I didn't see that."

Dallas chuckled. "Seriously, babe. Miranda's a raging bitch. I doubt there's anyone on this planet who'll feel sorry for her. She deserved to be humiliated on TV."

Callie crossed her arms over her chest. "You guys are clueless. I know how horrible Miranda is, and believe me, I wanted to smack her a few times myself, but this is *Miranda* we're talking about. Conniving and evil doesn't begin to cover what that woman's capable of." She sighed. "You're going to pay for this, Justin. One way or another, she won't let you get away with it."

I'd thought about that, and I didn't give a shit. I wasn't afraid of what she or her rich daddy would do to me. Shrugging, I started toward the pub and they followed. "I'll be fine. I don't care what she says about me to the tabloids. We all know it won't be true."

Cameras flashed and reporters moved in a frenzy as we walked up the sidewalk. Unfortunately, they weren't the only ones waiting on me. Miranda charged through them, coming straight at me, her high heels tapping on the cement.

"Incoming," Dallas said, voice low.

I knew what was coming before it even happened. Miranda reared her hand back and slapped me hard across the cheek. Callie fumed, but Dallas held her tight. I wasn't about to let my pregnant sister stand up for me. It was my mess.

Miranda poked a finger in my chest. "You're not getting the last word in here, I am. How dare you do this to me?" There were no tears in her eyes, only vengeance.

The cameramen moved in closer. "Simple," I replied with a shrug. "Our contract is done. I'm not obligated to stay with you anymore."

Her eyes widened in anger. "You're going to regret this."

"Oh, believe me, I already have."

She stormed away, and the reporters went crazy, thrusting microphones in my face. "Justin, what do you mean about being obligated to stay with Miranda? What kind of contract was it?" It was the same questions, over and over. I'd already revealed more than I should have, given my contract with the television station.

I held up my hand and continued walking. "Thanks for coming out tonight."

As soon as we got inside the pub, I breathed a sigh of relief. It was a private party, so the reporters weren't allowed inside. Callie grabbed my arm and nodded over at Corey, our brother, and my agent. He sat at the bar with Callie's best friend, Hannah, and one of our rookies and my friend, Cliff Stanford.

"You need to give Corey a heads-up about what just happened. He's the one who'll be handling this PR nightmare."

The thought deflated me a bit. I didn't want to bring trouble down on my brother. "Hopefully, it'll all be blown over by the time I get back into town."

Dallas slapped a hand on my shoulder. "Wishful thinking, buddy."

Groaning, I walked over to Corey. Cliff stood, grinning from ear to ear. "Good game tonight, bro. I hate I can't go to Wyoming with you. I was looking forward to some downtime."

I shook his hand. "Thanks, man. You'll have to come visit for a few days if you get a chance." I'd offered Cliff a room at my ranch for the summer, but his dad had some medical issues so he decided to go up to Vermont to be with his family instead.

He blew out a heavy sigh. "Hopefully, I can. If not, I'll see you in August." He patted my arm and smiled. "Take care."

Corey watched him walk off and shook his head. "I hate his dad's not doing well."

I sat down beside him. "Yeah, it's definitely messed him up. I know of something that'd make him happy, though." Since Cliff didn't have an agent, I'd hinted at Corey to take on the job.

Hannah snickered, and Corey gave me a sideward glance. "If you're referring to me being his agent, I offered to represent him."

That made me happy. "Thanks, brother. However, you're going to hate me after what I'm about to tell you." Corey was thirty-one years old, and a twin to my brother Brant, who was officially still one of my agents, but he had moved back to Minnesota to be with his now-wife.

Corey tossed a peanut in his mouth and turned to me, grinning devilishly. "No need to explain. I already know I'll have my work cut out for me while you're gone."

With a heavy sigh, I closed my eyes. "I'm sorry. I didn't think of all the shit you'd have to deal with."

He tossed another peanut into his mouth and shrugged. "Not worried in the least. You have a lot of people who love you out there."

I laughed, but there was no humor in it. "And a lot who don't," I added. The bartender came up and I ordered my usual: whiskey, straight up.

Corey waved me off. "There'll be a lot of shade coming your way, but you'll come out on top. Who knows," he said, nudging me with his elbow, "with all the exposure, you might get the movie deal you've always dreamed about."

"Doubt it. I'm not even sure that's what I want anymore. Hockey is who I am." The bartender set my tumbler of whiskey down, and I tossed it back, loving the smooth burn as it slid down my throat.

"True, but you have to think about what you're going to do

after you retire. You're twenty-nine years old. You have maybe ten years left and that's it, but only if you don't get hurt."

In my mind, it was hard to imagine giving up hockey for good. If I had my way, I'd play until I was fifty. But that wasn't the way the world worked. Eventually, I'd have to give it up and move on to something else. Acting was my second passion, but after Miranda got done smearing my name, that dream would be squashed. I had no doubt her father would make sure of that.

A set of hands slapped down on my shoulders from behind. "What's up, cuz? Break any more hearts in the last hour?" Maddox squeezed my shoulders, and I turned around. His wife, Lacey, also pregnant, stood beside him, trying her best to smile, but I knew she was miserable. Cheeks red from the June heat, she had her blonde hair pulled high and was wearing a light blue maternity sundress. Their baby was two weeks late. Ever since her brother married my sister, I considered her family.

"I break hearts all the time, what are you talking about?" I replied with a chuckle. I looked over at Lacey. "How you feeling?"

Snorting, she glanced down at her stomach. "Tired and ready for Maddox Jr. to come out. He's hard-headed like his daddy."

Maddox grinned and kissed her on the cheek. "You still love me."

An unfamiliar feeling washed over me—jealousy. Looking around the room at my teammates, a lot of them were in serious relationships or married with families of their own. I didn't have any of that. Having been stuck with Miranda for the past year, I couldn't. For the first time in my life, I wanted someone I could be serious with. Unfortunately, it didn't look like it was going to happen anytime soon.

"Where's Braeden and Sophia?" I asked Lacey.

A wide grin spread across her face as she glanced over at Maddox. He smiled and nodded. "Might as well tell him. It's about to be public anyway," he said.

I held up a hand. "Please don't tell me he's retiring, too." Sheepishly, Lacey bit her lip, and I had my answer. "Dammit, guys! There's not going to be anyone left other than me and Dallas."

Lacey snickered. "My brother's good at keeping the guys in line. You two will be great leaders."

I'd just joined the Charlotte Strikers, and now everyone was starting new adventures. I felt like I was the only one not moving on to the next stage in my life. I couldn't imagine giving up hockey like they were, when they had so many good years left.

"So what's golden boy going to be doing now that he's quitting?" I asked.

Lacey pulled out her phone and showed me a picture of Braeden proposing to Sophia in front of a tropical waterfall. "Braeden's a smart guy," Lacey added. "He used to fly up to New York to help me study for my medical exams. I always thought he'd make a good doctor, and I knew deep down that's what he wanted to be. It all came so easy to him."

Shock couldn't begin to describe how I felt. "Seriously? He's going to be a doctor?"

She nodded excitedly. "As soon as he finishes school. He has a long way to go, but that's why he decided to take summer courses up in New York. He'll be gone the rest of the summer."

"Well, shit," I announced. "Good for him." I looked around the room at all my teammates and sighed. So many changes.

A whistle echoed through the pub, and Kellan hopped up on one of the chairs. "Now that everyone's here, I just want to say how proud I am of this team. Being your coach has been the dream of a lifetime." He held up his beer. "To another winning season." The room burst out in cheers, and everyone drank to the upcoming season. Kellan turned his attention to Maddox and waved him up. "As you all know, this was Maddox's last game. I'm sure he has some things he'd like to say to you all."

Maddox helped Lacey sit down and kissed her before taking his place on the chair. I'd never seen him so happy. He stared out at the crowd and sighed. "I just want to say thank you for making this last season one of the best. I know I was a dick to a lot of you over the years."

Some of the guys snorted, and the room erupted into laughter. Maddox was a dick to a lot of the rookies. Back when Kellan was on the team, Maddox had gotten his ass kicked because of it. After he met Lacey, everything changed. He knew he had to be a better man for her.

"Okay, okay, I was worse than a dick," he corrected. "You'll have to thank my wife for putting me in my place."

"Got that right," I called out. I winked over at Lacey, and she smiled, but it soon disappeared. She grabbed her stomach, and I pushed my way over to her. "Lacey, you okay?"

By this time, it'd caught everyone's attention. Maddox ran through the crowd and knelt down beside her. "Babe, what's wrong?"

She stood, and that was when we noticed the small puddle on the floor. "I think this is about to be an even bigger night for you."

Maddox's face lit up and he shouted in delight. "Hell fucking yeah! I'm going to be a dad!" He kissed Lacey again and put his arm around her waist.

I stood on her other side and helped him. "All right, everyone! Looks like we're taking this party to the hospital." Maddox looked over at me, and I smiled. "Congratulations, Maddox."

CHAPTER TWO

MEGHAN

"I'M GONNA MISS YOU, MOMMY." Ellie sniffled, and it broke my heart. Tears burned in my eyes as I hugged my little eight-year-old princess. I was going to miss her more than anything.

"I'll miss you too, Ellie-Bear." I kissed her head and breathed her in. She smelled like coconut sunscreen. My father waved at me and pointed at Ellie. "I think Paw Paw's ready to toss you into the pool again." He always knew how to make her happy; he also knew how to distract her. A big smile spread across her face, and I kissed her cheek. "I'll be back before you know it."

She raced over to my dad, and he tossed her into the pool. My two nieces jumped in, and they all splashed each other.

"Don't worry, she'll be okay," my sister said, her voice coming from somewhere behind me.

I glanced at her over my shoulder. Kimberly was five years

older than me and married, with two girls. She had the auburn hair like our father, and I got the dark brown hair from our mother. We always spent summers in Nags Head at my parents' beach house. Us both being teachers gave us the privilege of having the summers off. "I know. This place is like a second home to her."

Kimberly nodded and breathed in the fresh, ocean air. "That it is. I'm starting to think we should all move out here. Give us a break from all the snowy winters."

I shook my head. "That's the best part. I love the snow."

She patted my arm like she felt sorry for me. "We're sisters, but yet, we're completely different."

That made me laugh. "Have you ever thought that it might be *you* that's not normal? Being snowed in is fun. I have Ellie to keep me company."

She snorted. "Being snowed in is one thing, but being stuck with my grumpy husband is another. I love him, but he's no fun stuck at home when he needs to be at work." Her husband, Jackson, was a workaholic. A lot of times it put him in a bad mood from all the stress. It was good money, and I know he did it for the family since a teacher's salary wasn't the best in the world. Kimberly often spent the summers with us while he stayed back in Wyoming. It gave her daughters something to do since they hardly ever saw their father. "What are you going to do over the next few weeks, all alone at your ranch?"

I shrugged. "Find someone to fix my fence and paint my barn. I'll probably call Grant and hang out with him some, too. Get some hiking in. He'll be happy to have me home, since I'm usually always here in the summers."

She shook her head and laughed. "When I first saw you with him, I was so happy. I thought you were moving on … until I found out he was gay."

I'd graduated high school with Grant. It wasn't until

college that he came out. I'd had a feeling long before that, but he never let on and it wasn't my business so I left it alone. He was a good friend, and I enjoyed being around him. Plus, he loved Ellie, and she loved him—and the treats he always brought her. His mother owned a bakery, so he always had access to the good stuff.

My mother walked out of the house, carrying a plate of sandwiches. "You're going to miss all the fun," she teased.

I rolled my eyes, and laughed. "I'll be back in a few weeks. I have a lot of work to do at the ranch. Been putting it off for years, and it's time I got my butt in gear."

Expression sad, she set the plate of sandwiches down on the picnic table. "I know, sweetheart. Trey had big plans for that place. It'll be nice to see it fixed up."

My chest tightened. "Yes, it will."

Trey was my husband for only two months before he was killed in action in Afghanistan. I'd found out I was pregnant the day before he left. He was so happy. Seeing his excitement and hearing all his stories about how he was going to give his daughter everything he never had were engrained in my mind. Even though he didn't know she was going to be a girl, he was convinced that was what our baby was going to be.

Looking at my daughter, I could see him in her golden amber eyes, and in the way she smiled. Other than that, she looked exactly like me. It broke my heart that she never got to meet Trey. Every time she asked about him, I'd show videos of him that we'd recorded over the years. Her favorite was our wedding.

I hugged my sister, and then my mother last, trying my best not to cry. I'd never been away from my daughter for so long at one time. "I'll call you when I get to Wyoming."

CHAPTER THREE

JUSTIN

"You already there?" Maddox asked.

I looked out the small, rounded airplane window and took in the snow-topped mountains surrounding Jackson Hole Airport. As we eased to a stop, I could hear the sounds of the pilot flipping switches in the cockpit and responding to crackling air traffic control directions.

"Yep. Took a private jet." In the background, I could hear his son's tiny cries; it made me smile. "How does it feel to be a father?"

Maddox chuckled. "Dude, it's an amazing feeling."

"I bet." As much as I wanted to get away from everything, I couldn't help but feel isolated and disconnected from the important things in my life. "You've gotta send me pictures. I hate I'm not there."

"Don't worry, I will. I have a question, though."

"What?"

"How do you expect to spend the summer in Wyoming without people recognizing you? You're the reigning America's Sexiest Bachelor right now, and I have no doubt your debacle with Miranda was all over TV last night. The second someone knows who you are, your picture's going to be all over the internet and then – boom! – no more secret hideout."

Running a hand through my hair, I groaned. In my bag there was a University of Wyoming baseball cap that I'd purchased online and a pair of dark sunglasses. "I brought my Hollywood disguise kit: sunglasses and a hat. Besides, I highly doubt anyone's going to realize who I am. And if they do, I can just pretend to be someone else."

Maddox burst out laughing. "Good luck with that." More voices echoed in the background, and I recognized his mother's voice. "Hey, my parents just got here to see the baby. We'll talk soon, okay?"

"Sounds good."

"Have fun out there, man. Might be a good thing you're not here – either the paparazzi are camped outside to get a peek at Maddox Jr. when we leave, or they're here to try to see you."

I slipped on my UW cap, hoping it would help me blend in and conceal my face a bit. "Sorry, man."

"It's okay. I know how to hip check someone if they get too close." We said our goodbyes, and I tossed my phone into my bag. The pilot, James, opened the cockpit door and stood with his flight attendant, waiting patiently. He'd flown me all over for the last five years.

Grabbing my bag, I slung it over my shoulder and walked to the exit. Another plane had landed, and people were getting off of it. I waited for them all to go inside the airport before leaving the plane. James extended his hand. "As always, it was a pleasure, Mr. Davis."

I shook his hand. "Thank you. I'll see you in eight weeks."

James nodded. "Until then."

Slipping on my sunglasses, I walked down the stairs and headed toward the small airport building, which was constructed with stacked stone and huge timbers to give a lodge-like feel. Glancing around, I saw a line of people waiting at the rental car counter. The last thing I wanted to do was stand around and give people a chance to figure out who I was. Instead of waiting with them, I walked out the front doors and set my bag on the ground. I'd gotten out here anonymously, but I'd failed to think about a car.

Pulling out my phone, I typed up a text to send to my family so they'd know I made it to Wyoming safely. Before I could hit send, a woman's voice came from behind, followed by a yelp as she slammed into my back and dropped her suitcase. I pitched forward from the impact, my sunglasses clattering to the sidewalk.

"Oh my God! I'm so sorry," she apologized, rushing over to pick up my sunglasses. *Fuck me.* Frozen in place, I said nothing, knowing that once she saw my face, my hopes of anonymity would be diminished. "Mom, I'll call you later tonight. Just wanted you to know I got back safely." She pocketed her phone in her fantastically short denim shorts and snatched my sunglasses off the ground. I wanted to grab my glasses out of her hand and slip them on, but the second her crystal-blue eyes focused in on mine, I couldn't think of anything other than how beautiful she was. She was around my age, and I noted there wasn't a certain ring on a significant left-hand finger. With dark brown hair in a messy bun and sun-kissed skin underneath her bright green tank top, she looked like she'd just gotten back from the beach. She stared at me for a few seconds, and I could've sworn there was recognition on her face, but then it dissipated as she held out my sunglasses. "I am so sorry for bumping into you. I have a habit of tripping over my own feet."

I took the glasses and slipped them on. "It's okay."

She held out her hand. "Since I fell all over you, might as well tell you my name. I'm Meghan."

Something inside me told me not to lie, so I shook her hand. "Justin." I wasn't about to give her my last name. Her grip was firm, and I liked it. "It's nice to meet you, Meghan."

"Bet you wouldn't be saying that if I broke your expensive sunglasses," she said with a smirk.

I let her hand go, loving the feel of how soft they were. "True. I'd be collecting if you did."

Her laugh made me smile even more. "So do you go to the university?" she asked, nodding at my hat.

Breathing a sigh of relief, I smiled. She didn't know who I was. "No. I'm just visiting the area."

Her smile widened. "I can tell you're not a native. Where are you from?"

If she didn't know who I was, I didn't see a reason to lie about where I lived. "Born in Minnesota, but live in North Carolina."

"North Carolina's a nice state. My parents have a house in Nags Head. I always enjoy going out there." Taking a deep breath, she glanced out at the mountains. "But as much as I like it, it's not home. If you ever decide to attend the University of Wyoming, it's a good school. I graduated a few years ago from there." She grabbed the handle of her suitcase and lifted it upright.

"I'll keep that in mind," I replied, watching her pull out her car keys.

She followed my line of sight down to her keys, and then met my gaze. "Are you waiting for a ride?"

With a shrug, I pointed inside at the rental car counter. "I was hoping to rent a car, but it looks like I might have to wait a while."

I could tell the wheels in her head were turning as she peered inside and then back at me. "Where you headed to?"

Blowing out a heavy sigh, I nodded off into the distance. "About thirty minutes out that way. It's called Southfork Ranch. I bought it, but I haven't seen it in person yet." My brother had found it, and I'd bought it under his name so the previous owners wouldn't know it was mine.

Her face lit up. "Seriously? That's right next to my place. You'll love it. Before the owners put it on the market, they asked if I wanted to buy it, but I couldn't afford it."

"I'm sorry," I replied.

She waved me off. "It's okay. I have enough to deal with at my own ranch." Taking a deep breath, she let it out slow and then bit her lip. "If you need a ride to Southfork, you can come with me. But if you turn into an ax murderer, I want you to know that I am skilled with a gun, and I do have one on me."

Barking out a laugh, I held up my hands. I really liked her. "You have nothing to worry about. If anything, I should be the one worried about getting in the car with you." Imagine my chances of survival if I got stuck in a car with a psychotic fan. Meghan didn't strike me as the crazy-bitch type, but you never knew for sure.

Meghan snickered and waved for me to follow her. "Come on." I followed her to a silver Toyota 4Runner, the tailgate slowly opening up as we approached. "You can put your stuff back here if you want," she said, tossing her suitcase inside.

I set my bag beside hers and got in her car. Sitting so close to her, I could smell her perfume. It reminded me of strawberries and sunshine. Rolling my eyes at my stupidity, I turned to the window. What the hell was wrong with me? I was used to having any woman I wanted, but I couldn't do that here. I wasn't a famous hockey player or the bachelor from *Rich and Single* right now; I needed to be just Justin.

"Hopefully, your husband or boyfriend won't mind you carting a stranger around," I said, watching her response carefully for clues.

Her eyes stayed on the road, but there was no mistaking the sadness I saw on her face. "It'll be fine. I'm more than capable of taking care of myself." It wasn't exactly the answer I was looking for, but I had a feeling it was a sore subject.

We pulled out onto the main highway, and I was amazed at all the open land that suddenly stopped at a towering mountain. These peaks weren't like the ones in North Carolina – ours were smaller, rounded clusters, and definitely not snowcapped in June.

"It's beautiful, isn't it?" Meghan murmured. She looked at me and smiled.

"It is," I agreed.

"What made you want to buy a ranch out here?"

I shrugged. "To get away, I guess. I've always wanted to come out this way, but never got the chance. Thought I'd do a little bit of fishing and hiking." I needed somewhere I could disappear for a while.

We turned off the main highway onto a more secluded road. Passing by all the different ranches and farms reminded me of a Western movie. "Are you going to stay out here permanently, or is the ranch a summer home of sorts?" she asked.

"Summer and vacation home for now. When I'm not living there, I'm sure my family and friends will enjoy using it for vacation."

Her eyebrows rose. "Must be nice. What exactly do you do for a living? Has to be lucrative to afford a place like Southfork."

And there it was, the beginning of the questions I didn't want to answer. Putting on my dashing smile, I faced her.

"Getting a little too personal, aren't we? I don't think I know you well enough to answer that question."

With a small snicker, she shook her head. "Fine, you don't have to answer. But if you're a drug dealer and I get caught with you, I'm going to say you kidnapped me." We both laughed, and I realized it was the first time I'd ever truly felt comfortable with a woman that wasn't related to me. Maybe it was because she didn't know who I was, and so I could just be myself. Time passed by quickly, and I knew we had to be getting closer to my ranch. It was fun watching Meghan smile as she pointed out all the animals we passed. She even gave me the low down on all the best restaurants to try. Unfortunately, I wasn't going to be able to go to any of them. "All right, we're almost to Southfork." She slowed the car and pointed off to the left. "Down there is my ranch. Your land is right across from me." The sign over her ranch's entrance read *Harvest Moon Ranch*. I didn't get a good look at anything else before she turned down my dirt road.

It was exactly what you'd imagine a typical ranch entrance would look like, with the big wooden poles to the sides with the one across the top, and a sign that said *Southfork Ranch* hanging from it. I had some ideas on how I wanted to modify the entrance, but that had to wait for another time.

Meghan sucked in a breath and sighed. "I haven't been down this road in years. It still takes my breath away."

Even I was surprised at how amazing it was. There was nothing but open fields, surrounded by a wooden fence as far as you could see on both sides of the road. I had five hundred acres all to myself, with my own lake and stream that stretched through a mile and a half of my property. The Grand Teton National Park adjoined my land, giving me all the access I needed to do my fishing and hiking. I didn't have to leave my ranch if I didn't want to. It was all part of my seclusion plan.

Meghan pulled up to the house and clicked the tailgate lift. I opened my door and stepped out, leaning back in to face her. "Thanks for the ride. I really appreciate it."

Grinning wide, she shrugged. "Hey, it's the least I can do."

I nodded toward my new home. "Want to take a tour with me?"

Her eyes lit up like she wanted to, but then she sighed and shook her head. "Not today. I really need to get to the grocery store, or I won't have any food at my house."

I couldn't let her leave without knowing I'd see her again. "I understand. Maybe next time?"

She nodded. "Definitely." Reaching into her glove compartment, she tore a piece of paper off a pad and wrote down her number. "Give me a call if you need anything. I'm just across the road."

Our fingers touched as I took the paper. "I'll be sure to do that."

After grabbing my bag out of the back, I watched her drive away. Wyoming was already off to a great start.

CHAPTER FOUR

MEGHAN

Justin Davis. Famous center forward for the Charlotte Strikers, and he was living right across the street. And to top it off, he was America's Sexiest Bachelor, who just dumped his fiancée on television for everyone to see.

Heart racing, I sped down Justin's road and across the street. As soon as I came to a stop outside my cabin, I whipped out my phone, fingers trembling. I jumped out of my car and paced around, line ringing. "Come on, come on. Answer the phone."

"I'm here," Kimberly laughed. "What's wrong?"

I closed my eyes, envisioning Justin's face. I knew I was right. "Wrong isn't the word I'd use. But maybe the fact that Justin Davis bought Southfork Ranch, and I gave him a ride from the airport, is something worth getting a little excited about."

"What?" she screamed. "You're joking, right?"

I shook my head, knowing very well she couldn't see me. "Shh … don't tell anyone. I don't think he wants anyone to know he's here."

She snorted. "I can see why. The paparazzi have been on him like the plague since he dumped Miranda on live TV."

"And what better way to disappear than to come here?" I added. But what were the odds of that?

"Are you sure he's Justin Davis?"

Even I started doubting myself, but he looked exactly like him, and he said he was from Minnesota and North Carolina. It all added up. "Pretty sure," I said. "I asked him what he did for a living, and he very quickly deflected the question. I just pretended he was a normal guy. He seemed to relax more when he thought I didn't know who he was."

Kimberly chuckled. "This is insane. I can't believe you gave him a ride."

I wasn't in the habit of letting a stranger get in my car, so I was pretty confident it was him. "He didn't want to be anywhere near the people in the airport. When I realized who he was, I kind of figured out he didn't want to be recognized. That's why I offered to take him home."

"I am so jealous of you right now. But don't tell Jackson that," she said, snickering. "What now? Do you think you'll see him again?"

Grabbing my bag out of the back of my car, I headed inside. It was going to be strange being home by myself, without Ellie. I missed her so much already. At least the Justin excitement had helped take my mind off that. "Most likely not. I did casually give him my phone number, in case he needed anything, but I highly doubt he'll use it. He's famous, for Christ's sake."

"That doesn't mean anything."

A car door slammed outside, and I rushed over to the window. "Kim, I have to go. Emmett and Cody are here."

"Okay. Tell them I said hey."

"Will do." We hung up, and I hurried to the door. Cody was just about to hit the doorbell when I opened the door. "Well, if it isn't my hired hand who's ditching me to study abroad this summer."

Cody sheepishly shrugged and held out his arms. "I still love you, Aunt Meg."

"You better." Laughing, I hugged him hard. He reminded me so much of Trey. They had the same amber-colored eyes with gold specks, and floppy, light brown hair. Even Emmett shared the same traits. "It's okay, though. Not everyone gets to experience that sort of thing, especially ones in high school."

I let him go, and he winked. "Looks good on college applications."

"Yeah, I bet that's the only reason." Chuckling, he hurried off to the kitchen like he always did. "Good luck finding something in there," I shouted. "I haven't been to the store yet."

Grinning wide, Emmett shook his head. "I'm glad we caught you in time. He has to be at the airport in an hour." He opened up his arms, and hugged me. I loved being around Emmett and Cody because they reminded me so much of Trey, but on the other hand, it hurt to look at them sometimes. They all shared the same eye color, but Emmett had the same build and facial features. Most people used to think he and Trey were twins, but Emmett was two years older.

"He's going to have a blast," I said, letting him go.

With a heavy sigh, he nodded. "I have no doubt. I'm sorry he's not going to be here to help with the fence. I can find someone else to do it."

I shook my head. "Don't go doing that now," I scolded. "You of all people know I can take care of myself. I'm sure I can find someone."

His gaze narrowed in concern. "When my brother left to go overseas, I promised him I'd look out for you."

I squeezed his arm. "And you have. But there comes a time when I have to do things for myself. Trey's been gone eight years now. I can't rely on you forever. You have your own family to take care of." His wife, Samantha, was one of my closest childhood friends so I knew she didn't mind Emmett looking out for me. She was the one who'd introduced me to Trey. Over the past couple of years, she'd made it her life's mission to find me someone else. Guess you could say she was the town matchmaker.

Emmett's expression saddened. "It has been eight years, but you're showing no signs of moving on."

"Seriously, Emmett. Just because I'm not dating anyone doesn't mean I'm stuck. I've had Ellie to think about. She keeps me busy." Maybe part of that was a lie, but it wasn't that I didn't want to move on. I just wasn't attracted to any of the men that came my way.

Emmett didn't believe me by the look on his face. "Keep telling yourself that, Meghan. With Ellie gone for the next few weeks, you should take some time to focus on yourself." His eyes lit up. "Hey, we're having a summer get-together at our house in a couple of weeks. All the guys from work will be there. Why don't you come? Might be a great way for you to meet new people." Emmett was a park ranger for the Grand Teton National Park. I'd already met some of the guys he worked with, and I got along with them great, but not in a romantic kind of way.

I gave in. "Fine. I'll be there."

Cody came back in the room, carrying a handful of chocolate chip cookies. "All right, I'm ready to go."

I chuckled. "Looks like it." I hugged him again. "Be safe in Spain, Cody. Don't do anything stupid. You'll be missed around here."

He shoved a cookie into his mouth. "Tell Ellie I'll see her when I get back."

"I will." Letting him go, it took all I had not to cry. Cody had been a huge help to me, not only with the ranch, but with Ellie. She loved spending time with him. He was the big brother she never had.

Cody's eyes saddened. "I really am sorry I won't be here this summer."

I kissed his forehead. "Don't worry, I'll have plenty of stuff for you to do when you get back."

Emmett hugged me again. "Call me if you need anything."

"Will do." I walked with them out to Emmett's truck and watched them drive away. Something inside me felt different, but I couldn't figure out what it was. All I knew was that things were about to change, only I didn't know how.

CHAPTER FIVE

JUSTIN

"DUDE, YOUR FACE IS EVERYWHERE right now."

Cliff was not telling me anything I didn't know. I had the evidence on my laptop, my own face looking back at me. As much as I wanted to believe the world had forgotten, it wasn't so. I closed my laptop and sighed. "This is a nightmare."

Cliff chuckled. "For you, yeah, but I think your bitch of an ex-fiancée is loving the spotlight."

"Of course she is. Guess it's a good thing I don't plan on leaving my ranch. How's your dad doing?"

His chuckles turned silent. "Okay, for now. He had two stents put in his heart. He'll probably have to have surgery soon. I'm taking over the garage until I can hire someone to take my place. It's a good thing I grew up working on cars."

When I wasn't stuck around Miranda, I'd helped him build the engines on some of his classic cars. I'd enjoyed it. "Let me know if you need help up there. I'll fly to Vermont anytime."

"Thanks, dude. Business has been a little slow, so I think I'm okay. Besides, you have the cowboy life to live out there. It's a shame you can't go out and meet some Wild West chicks, what with you staying anonymous."

Thoughts of Meghan ran through my mind. Looking out the large bay window in my kitchen, I could barely see the entrance to her ranch. "I met one, actually."

"Oh yeah? Did she jump and scream when she realized who you were?"

A smile lit up my face. "Not at all. She doesn't know who I am. I met her at the airport, and she gave me a ride to my ranch."

He snorted. "And she didn't know who you were? Where she been living . . . under a rock?"

I burst out laughing. "Turns out she lives on a ranch across the road from mine. I'm glad she doesn't know who I am. It was nice being able to be normal." Her phone number sat on my kitchen table and I picked it up. It was only just yesterday since I met her, but I wanted to call her. The only problem was that the more time I spent with her, the harder it was going to be to keep my identity a secret.

"Are you going to see her again?" Cliff asked.

Blowing out a sigh, I sat down at the table. "I want to, but I don't know if it's a good idea. Especially with the shitstorm going on about me right now. If someone sees us together, it could cause her problems."

"So don't let anyone see you together. Simple as that."

A part of me wondered if it could be possible. The media didn't know where I was, and they definitely weren't going to go looking in Wyoming. Miranda had no clue I loved hiking or fishing. The first place she'd think to look would be somewhere like Malibu. I was safe for now.

"We'll see," I replied. "I've been lucky so far. Had my

groceries delivered this morning. Didn't even have to see the person."

Cliff chortled. "Better than getting mobbed at the grocery store. Those shelves would be full of tabloids with your face on them." True. And it'll probably be like that until I flew back to Charlotte.

"All right, man, I'm hopping off of here. Remember to call me if you need help."

"Got it. Enjoy your alone time. Honestly, I don't see how you're going to survive being all by yourself."

"I'll figure it out." We hung up, and I looked down at Meghan's number. Grabbing my brand-new cowboy hat, I placed it on my head. If I was going to live on a ranch, I had to play the part.

I'd made my decision.

Instead of calling her, I trekked down my long, dirt driveway to the road. It was late afternoon, so I had no clue if she was going to be home. I'd spent the whole morning ordering fishing rods and hiking gear and walking around my land. There was still a lot of ground I hadn't covered.

There was no one in sight down either lane as I crossed over to Harvest Moon Ranch. Meghan's ranch was smaller than mine, and it needed a little bit of work. The fence was old and falling apart, and the paint on the barn was peeling off in large strips. She had a few cows, but no sight of horses or any other animals. Her cabin was smaller than mine, but quaint, with a sleek, green tin roof.

Her voice echoed from the backyard, and a part of me didn't want to intrude, but I wanted to see her. I followed the sound of her voice around the side of the house, and once I saw her, dressed in a pair of denim shorts, a sleeveless plaid shirt, and boots, I couldn't take my eyes off of her.

CHAPTER SIX

MEGHAN

"You're already booked up for the summer?" Patience was not a virtue of mine, especially when I was dead set on getting my ranch fixed up, once and for all. I'd put it off way too long. Finding a handyman to work on my fence had turned into a nightmare. Everyone I knew to call was busy.

"I'm sorry, Meghan," George replied, sounding sincere. "We've never had so much work to do. It's a good thing, but I hate we can't help you out."

George was a friend of my father who owned a contracting business. He had a group of guys who worked under him, and I was hoping one of them would be free. "It's okay, George. I'm sure I'll find someone to fix the fence." The last thing I wanted to do was put an ad out in the paper for help. I didn't want someone I didn't know working around my house.

Huffing, I sat down on my favorite canopy swing and

marked George's name off on my list. "This sucks," I grumbled, crumpling up the paper.

"Is this a bad time?" a voice called out. Grabbing my chest, I jumped out of the swing. Justin appeared off to the side, holding out his hands. "Shit. I'm sorry. Didn't mean to scare you."

Taking a deep breath, I let it out slow, my heart racing ninety miles an hour. Mainly because it was Justin Davis, famous hockey player and reality star. At my house. Not to mention he looked like the sexiest cowboy I'd ever seen, dressed in worn out jeans, boots, and a cowboy hat. I had to blink twice to make sure it was him. First and foremost, I had to remain calm and collected. I wasn't the type to shriek and squeal because someone famous was within touching distance. "It's okay. I just wasn't expecting company."

He walked up to me, his gaze on the surrounding mountains. "I don't think I'll ever get tired of this."

"There are mountains in North Carolina," I quipped.

"Yes, but not like this." His eyes met mine, and my heart fluttered. There was no denying how gorgeous he was in person. For my own sake, I had to keep those thoughts out of my head.

Clasping my hands in front of me, I fiddled with my fingers. It was an unfortunate nervous habit. "Did you need me for something?" I asked.

He averted his gaze back to the mountains and shrugged. "Well … I spent yesterday exploring my ranch and realized I want some farm animals. However, I don't know the first thing about raising them." He smiled at me. "Thought maybe you'd have some pointers for me."

Sighing, I nodded toward my vacant barn. "I wish I did, but I don't have any animals other than the two cows in the field. I did have a horse, but it was too expensive to keep him."

My parents had offered to help pay for him, but I refused to take their money. Ellie was heartbroken.

Justin stared at me, his gaze concerned. I wasn't expecting to see that. "I'm sorry."

I shrugged. "It's okay. I'm a teacher, so I don't exactly make a ton of money." I didn't mean for it to be a jab, but he had no clue how lucky he was.

He stepped closer. "You're a teacher, huh? What grade?"

Crossing my arms over my chest, I pursed my lips teasingly. "If I recall correctly, you wouldn't tell me what you did for a living. I don't think we know each other well enough for me to answer your question."

Chuckling, he stuck his thumbs in the pockets of his jeans, the perfect cowboy stance. "Good point."

I waved him off. "I'm just messing with you. I teach fifth grade."

A smile lit up his face. "I remember my fifth-grade teacher. Had the hugest crush on her."

That made me laugh. "I bet."

He smiled and shook his head, as if remembering those times. "So long ago."

"What? Like twelve years," I teased, knowing very well how old he was. Although, I was older than him by two years.

He smirked. "Close. More like eighteen. You've got to be around there as well."

I smirked back. "You'll never know."

Justin chuckled, and turned his attention to the old blue truck by the barn. "Nice truck, by the way. I've always wanted one like that but never found one I liked." It was my husband's, and he adored it. It hadn't run right in six years, but didn't have the heart to get rid of it.

"Do you want to take a look at it?" I asked.

His eyes lit up. "Hell yeah." He followed close beside me as we walked across my backyard to the barn. It was so strange being around him, knowing who he was. A part of me wanted to tell him that I knew, but I didn't want to break the spell. Being around him was intriguing.

The closer we got to the truck, the more excited he looked. It was like a kid at Christmas. You'd think a superstar like him would want brand new, shiny cars, but he genuinely appeared interested in the truck.

I patted the hood. "She ran like a top back in the day." He opened the driver side door and peeked inside, running his hands gently across the interior. "My husband loved her," I added, lost in memories.

He froze and then backed away, as if he was doing something wrong. "He's not going to charge out here and kick my ass for talking to you and touching his truck, is he?"

On the contrary, if Trey was still alive, he'd be getting Justin's autograph. He loved hockey. I shook my head. "Trey died eight years ago in Afghanistan. It was his second tour." I used to cry every time I talked about him, but now, I thinking about him gave me peace.

Sighing, Justin gently shut the truck door. "I'm so sorry, Meghan."

"You didn't know. We were married two months before he was killed in action." I nodded at the truck. "This was his baby. I've been having problems with it for years. The mechanics don't seem to know how to fix it."

Brows furrowed, Justin lifted the hood and studied the engine. I didn't know anything about fixing cars. He fiddled around with some of the different components, and then stepped back, staring at it as if in deep thought.

"What would you say if I said I thought I could fix it?" he asked.

That caught me by surprise. "Really?" I gasped, staring at him incredulously. Who would've thought he'd know how to fix cars?

Justin nodded, and shut the hood. "I have a friend who does mechanic work on the side. I helped him several times." He looked at me and winked. "He taught me a few tricks."

"I'd say go for it, then. Don't know what kind of luck you'll have getting it to run, but you're more than welcome to try."

He walked over to me, grinning devilishly. "How about we make a deal?"

Crossing my arms over my chest, I stared curiously at him. "What kind of deal?"

Keeping his eyes on mine, he nodded toward the truck. "If I can get it to run, I'll pay you to let me borrow it for the summer. Being that I don't have any wheels right now."

"Why don't you just rent a car?" I asked, wondering what he was going to say.

Nonchalantly, he shrugged as if it wasn't a big deal. "I'd rather do this." He held out his hand, waiting on me to seal the deal. If I agreed, that meant he'd be spending time at my ranch. Before I could shake his hand, he pulled back. "Oh, and another thing. I kind of overheard you on the phone earlier. If you want, I can help fix your fence."

It was too good to be true. I glanced around my yard to see if there were any hidden men with video cameras. The Justin I watched on *Rich and Single* was not the same Justin in front of me. He held out his hand again, and I shook it.

"Deal."

His grin broadened. "Excellent. Do you want me to start now or wait until tomorrow morning?"

I looked down at my phone. It was almost time. "Tomorrow morning sounds good. Right now, I have to get ready for my date."

His smile faltered, and he tipped his hat. "He's a lucky guy. I'll see you in the morning."

If he only knew. I watched him walk down my driveway and disappear across the road, my heart raced inexplicably.

Rushing inside, I set up my iPad on the table just as the call came through. Ellie's sweet, angelic face appeared on the screen, her hair still wet.

"Right on time for our date," I said happily.

She squealed and bounced in her seat. "Mommy, you won't believe what all I saw today at the aquarium."

Happiness filled me, and I couldn't contain my smile. "Tell me all about it. I have all day."

CHAPTER SEVEN

MEGHAN

"I CAN'T BELIEVE HE'S GOING to be at your house all day, every day," Kimberly gushed. "When are you going to tell him you know who he is?"

I finished scrambling up the eggs and slid them into a bowl. "I don't know. Probably soon. I don't like being sneaky like this. It feels deceitful. Then again, I don't want to ruin his secret."

"Who says you have to? If you tell him the truth, you can promise to stay quiet. Simple as that."

"Good point." Then maybe if the truth came out, he'd actually talk about his life. I was curious to know more about him. Right now, he kept it all to himself. Getting the inside scoop would be very interesting. I looked out the window, and there he was, walking up my driveway. "Kim, he's here. I have to go."

"Have fun, sis," she said in a sing-song voice. "I'm getting ready to walk with Ellie down to the beach."

"Tell my little Ellie-Bear I love her."

"I will. Talk to you later." We hung up, and I watched Justin walk the rest of the way up to my cabin. He had on a darker pair of jeans and an open plaid shirt with a white T-shirt underneath. Very different attire than the designer labels he wore on television. If he wanted to fit in with the locals, he was on the right track.

I opened up the kitchen door and waved him over. "Good morning."

His smile made my stomach flutter. "Morning. I hope it's not too early."

"Not at all. I've already been to the store this morning and made breakfast." And while I was at the store, I got to see all the tabloids about him and Miranda. I couldn't help but buy a couple of them. I'd spent part of the morning reading the stories, even though I knew about ninety-nine percent of them were untrue. I watched the whole season of *Rich and Single*. Miranda was a catty bitch who talked shit about the other women behind their backs. I wouldn't want her to be my friend ... or enemy.

Justin took in a deep breath. "I see that. I can smell the bacon from here."

"If you're hungry, you can come in and eat. I made plenty."

He paused for a second then nodded. "I think I will."

I held the door open for him, and he walked in, gazing around curiously at my kitchen. I'd remodeled it a few years ago with updated appliances, but it was nothing compared to the one at his ranch. However, I was happy with my two-bedroom cabin. It was the perfect size for Ellie and me.

Pulling out two plates, I handed one to Justin and nodded at the food. "Get what you want." I filled my plate and sat down at the table. Justin did the same and sat across the table, staring curiously at me. "What?" I asked.

He shrugged. "Are you always this nice to strangers?"

I took a bite of my biscuit, grinning smugly. "I told you I'm good with a gun. Besides, it's easier to be nice than mean. You haven't given me a reason not to be." It was sort of a lie. I wouldn't have allowed just any person into my home. He was a different story. What made him even more interesting was that he was actually a nice guy. He wasn't in front of a camera or putting on a show. He was in my kitchen, eating breakfast, and clearly enjoying it.

"These biscuits are so damn good." It took all I had in me not to laugh as he shoved the rest of the biscuit into his mouth and then grabbed another one.

"Glad you approve. My aunt used to make them every Sunday at our family get-togethers. At least, until my grandmother died."

He nodded as if he understood. He'd talked about his sister and some of his teammates while he was on *Rich and Single*. "My family's the same way. With my parents still in Minnesota, I don't see them much. Luckily, I have my sister and one of my brothers in North Carolina. We get together for meals pretty regularly." I liked that he was close to his family. At least, he wasn't lying to me, only not elaborating.

"I have a sister too," I added. "She's pretty much my best friend." I finished the last of my food and washed my plate off before sticking it in the dishwasher. Justin watched me and did the same with his plate once he was done eating.

He guzzled down a glass of orange juice and stretched his arms over his head. "All right, let's see what I can do with this."

We walked outside, and he followed me to the garage. Trey had every single tool you could imagine. Judging by Justin's reaction, he was impressed. He opened up the various roller cabinet drawers and shook his head. "Your husband had quite a collection," he said.

Leaning against the door frame, I glanced around the garage. It was Trey's domain. I couldn't remember the last time I'd stepped foot inside. "Trey loved fixing stuff. It's what he enjoyed."

"You miss him a lot?" he asked, glancing at me over his shoulder.

I nodded. "He was my high school sweetheart. We spent a lot of years together."

Sighing, he turned back to the tools. "I wouldn't know what that's like. All of my friends are getting married and starting families, and here I am … alone in Wyoming."

"You're not alone, Justin. You have me, a janky truck, and a broken-down fence to keep you company."

A sly smile spread across his face as he turned around. "That I do. It's just a shame you're taken. I'm sure whoever you had your date with last night wouldn't want you around another man."

The thought made me smile. If he only knew my date was with an eight-year-old princess. Ellie was young, but she knew who he was from catching glimpses of the show before going to bed. All she'd ever talked about was being a movie star. If she knew her mother was hanging out with one, she'd demand her grandparents fly her home immediately.

I waved him off and winked. "I'm a liberated woman."

Chuckling, Justin grabbed a handful of tools. "Okay. If he comes over and sees me here, I'm going to say you kidnapped me."

I hooted at his reference to our earlier conversation in the car. "You do that." I helped him carry the tools over to the truck. "Do you need anything else right now? Maybe a bottle of water?"

He took off his plaid shirt and the white T-shirt off underneath, exposing his washboard abs. "Nope, I'm good for now."

Rolling my eyes, I turned on my heel. He knew what he was doing. "I see that." That was the Justin I recognized from television. I took a step toward the house, but then a car door slammed out front. For a second, I froze, thinking I'd just imagined it, but that was when I heard Emmett's voice.

"Meg!"

I turned around so fast, I almost tripped over my own feet. "Shit!" I hissed. Justin quickly gathered up the tools and hid them behind the truck. I ran over to him and pushed him into the barn. "Hide and don't say a word."

"Who is it?" he asked.

Instead of answering, I rushed out the barn to my back-porch swing. Sweat dripped down my face, and I swiftly wiped it off just as Emmett turned the corner. "Hey," I called out, trying not to sound breathless.

He walked up the steps, carrying a plate of muffins, dressed in his ranger uniform. "Samantha wanted me to bring these to you. She was going to bring them herself, but she got called into the hospital early."

I stood and he handed me the plate. "They look amazing. I'll be sure to call her later."

Emmett searched around the yard. "I could've sworn you were talking to someone out here. Thought maybe you'd already found someone to fix the fence."

"I was talking to my sister on the phone. And you're right, I did find someone to fix the fence. He'll be working on it soon." I set the muffins down on my patio table.

Breathing a sigh of relief, he reached out and grabbed me in a one-armed hug. "That makes me happy. I'd talked to George earlier, and he told me his men were booked. I was just about to work on the damn thing myself."

He let me go, and I pursed my lips. "I told you I could

handle this on my own. I got it covered. Besides, you're always busy with work."

With a heavy sigh, he nodded. "I know. Don't be mad at me."

"I could never be mad at you, Emmett. Especially for wanting good things for me."

He squeezed my arm and nodded toward the front of the house. "I have to get to work. Don't forget to call Samantha. She's been missing you, especially now that Cody's gone."

"I will. Promise." Once Emmett was out of sight, I caught a glimpse of Justin in the barn, leaning against the entrance and watching me curiously. Holding my chest, I walked down to him when I heard Emmett drive away. "That was close."

Justin fiddled with the wrench in his hand. "Was that the guy you're seeing?" he asked, sounding all serious. It made no sense. Why would he even care? The guy dated models and movie stars … not someone like me. Even if he was interested in me, it would *never* work.

"No," I answered, gauging his reaction. He appeared to be relieved, but that couldn't be right. My heart jumped with the prospect of him being interested in me, but my brain told me to stay as far away from him as I could. Unfortunately, I didn't want to. "He's Trey's brother, Emmett," I explained. "His son was the one who was supposed to fix my fence this summer, but he got the opportunity to study abroad in Spain."

His smile widened. "Spain's a beautiful country. I went there a couple years ago."

"You're quite the traveler, aren't you?"

He shrugged and focused on the truck's engine, his hands already dirty from the muck under the hood. "You could say that. I like seeing the world."

"Sounds nice. I wish I could."

Justin's green eyes focused on me. "You can."

I shook my head. "I'm not like you, Justin. Our worlds are

completely different." Maybe it was my tone or the way I stared at him, but something clicked.

Stepping away from the truck, he slowly blew out a breath. "What are you implying?"

Playing games with him was not what I wanted. I didn't like pretending I didn't know who he was. "I think you know." I took a step toward him, fiddling with my fingers like I always did when I was nervous. It was hard not to be when he never took his eyes off of me. His stare was intense, full of life. That had to be one of the things women loved about him. I looked up at him and sighed. "I know who you are, Justin Davis. I knew the second I bumped into you at the airport."

CHAPTER EIGHT

JUSTIN

Jaw clenching, I closed my eyes. That was not what I wanted to hear. "I should've known this was too good to be true." I opened my eyes, not knowing what to expect when I looked at Meghan. What I saw was understanding, maybe even compassion. She took another step toward me, rubbing her hands nervously. I didn't want her to be nervous around me. "Have you told anyone?"

She bit her lip. "Only my sister, but she knows not to say anything. When I met you at the airport, I had a feeling you were trying to hide. After everything that happened with Miranda, I didn't want to bring attention to you."

I scoffed. "I'd imagine most women right now would be pissed at me."

"Are you kidding?" she gasped incredulously. "Your ex is a thundercunt. My sister and I didn't like her one bit." I smiled, and she held up her hand. "I'm not saying that dumping her on live television was the way to go, but I can say it needed to be done." It was a relief to hear her say that. Hopefully, the aftermath when I got back home wouldn't be so bad.

"What made you want to come clean now?" I asked.

A small smile spread across her face, and she looked off at the mountains. She was so fucking beautiful. "Believe me, it was kind of thrilling having you here and pretending you were just a normal guy. I haven't been comfortable around men much, not since my husband died." Her blue eyes met mine. "What I didn't like was you holding back. If you're going to be around me, I don't want you to feel like you have to lie." With a heavy sigh, she moved closer. "You're not the only one who wants to keep your whereabouts a secret."

I nodded in understanding. "Your boyfriend, right? Is that one of the reasons why you didn't want Emmett to see me?"

She burst out laughing. "Not at all. If anything, Emmett wants to see me with someone. He's making me come to a party at his house in a couple of weeks so I can meet some of the guys he works with."

A sharp pain exploded inside of me, and it took a few seconds to realize what it was ... jealousy. I didn't want her meeting other men. Hell, I hated the fact that she was already taken. "What about your boyfriend?" I asked. "If not for him, why would you care about keeping my secrets?"

She stared at me for a long second and then pulled out her phone. "My date last night was with someone special. I have another one tonight, and every night for the next few weeks." She held onto her phone for a few more seconds before showing it to me. There was a picture of her with a young girl with golden amber eyes and wavy brown hair. I could see the resemblance between them. "The reason I'm keeping you being here a secret is because I don't want my daughter dragged into the media shitstorm you have brewing right now.

It's not fair to her. Not to mention, I don't want my business being out there for the world to see, even if we are just friends. You, of all people, know how the media can skew things."

"I understand," I said. "And I don't blame you." She was the first woman I'd been around who didn't want to be in the public eye with me. It was for the best, anyway. She had her daughter to think about. I smiled at the picture. "She looks like you."

Meghan's smile brightened. "She's everything to me. Right now, she's spending the rest of summer in Nags Head with my family while I get the ranch in order. I promised her we'd video chat every day." She pocketed her phone. "That's who my date was with."

"So you're not seeing anyone right now that I should be worried about stopping by?" I asked.

She chuckled. "No. If you want to still work on the truck and the fence, I'd be extremely grateful. Having you around has definitely made this summer more exciting."

"I can agree with you on that." The whole purpose of coming to Wyoming was so I could be alone and enjoy the time away from the media. But I didn't want to be alone if Meghan and I could spend time together without having to worry. I'd never been able to enjoy my time anywhere without the media following me around. Meghan was the first genuine person I'd come across in a long time, even if she did know who I was and didn't tell me.

Meghan held out her hand. "Let's make a deal. We both keep our friendship a secret, and we both promise to be open and honest with each other. Because frankly, I have a lot of questions I want to ask to you."

I shook her hand but didn't let go. "You might not like the answers."

She snorted. "I can handle it. I watched you kiss a gazillion girls on *Rich and Single,* and pummel guys on the ice. Your whole life was on a show for the world to see."

I didn't like that she saw me like that. All she saw was a guy who put up a front just to make the show more appealing. There was more to me than she knew. "That's not how I really am, Meghan. You don't honestly think that, do you?"

"I don't know what to think," she said, shrugging. "I've never met someone like you before. Although, I will say I'm guilty of assuming. It's hard not to see your type as arrogant and devoid of any understanding of how the rest of the world lives."

It was like a slap in the face, but I was guilty of it. I'd never cared much about how other people lived. I'd only worried about my own life and how I could get ahead. Being in her home and hearing about her life made me aware that I could never have anything like that.

Slowly, she let go of my hand. "How can I make you see that I'm not like that?" I asked, voice low.

She looked up at me and smiled. "Just be yourself."

For the rest of the day, I worked on the truck while Meghan planted seeds in her garden. There were a lot of old parts on the truck that needed to be replaced. Once I ordered those up, I had no doubt I could get it running.

Every once in a while, Meghan would look over at me, and I'd look at her. There was a connection between us, but I knew not to pursue it, and it was obvious she wasn't going to either. I'd never had a female friend that didn't have the "benefits" attached. Meghan was going to be my first. Once the day was done, I headed back to my ranch.

Sitting on my back porch, I guzzled down a beer and propped my feet up on the railing. The sky had a pinkish glow from the sunset, and the air was brisk and cool. But in the distance, thunder rolled as a storm began to come in. I was starting to think I needed to spend every summer in Wyoming. The weather was significantly more tolerable than the oppressive North Carolina heat and humidity.

My phone rang, and I looked down at it to see Callie's name. "Hey," I answered.

"Hey, how's it going out there?"

"Pretty good. You're going to love the ranch. There's so much to do out here." I walked around to my vacant barn. The smell of horses still hung in the air. It was one of the things on my list to get.

"I can't wait to see it. Once the baby's born, I'll be able to fly again."

A flash of lightning raced across the sky. I moved further into the barn and sat down on a bale of hay. "How's everything going out there? You and the baby feeling okay?"

"We're doing great. Dallas and the guys are helping out with the junior hockey camp this week. I know the kids miss seeing you there."

That brought a smile to my face. I loved teaching young hockey players how to expand their craft. It was something I hoped to continue after I retired. There was no way I could give up hockey completely, even if I was old and gray.

"What about Miranda?" I asked, not really wanting to know. I'd intentionally stayed away from TV and the internet.

The line went silent for a few seconds, which wasn't good. "Well … she's hell bent on ruining your life, but you already knew that," she explained. "Then again, you have a lot of people sticking up for you."

"What is she saying?"

Callie huffed. "Basically, that you cheated on her. If it comes out that you did, you'll be faced with a lawsuit from the production company. It was in your contract that you couldn't engage in any activities with people of the opposite sex."

I was a fool for signing that fucking contract. At the time, Miranda was still a cunt, but I thought more with my dick than anything. She was wild as hell in the bedroom. "I didn't cheat on her stupid ass," I griped angrily.

The thunder rumbled overhead, and the rain started. It mimicked my mood. "I know, but there are women coming out of the woodwork, saying you slept with them. It isn't helping."

My insides shook with rage. I was angry at myself for being so stupid and doing the show when I knew it was rigged. "How many?"

She sighed. "Five, so far. I bet a million dollars Miranda's daddy is paying them off. Corey hired a private investigator to look into it."

"Good. Tell him I'll pay anything to get this shit handled." Corey handled a lot of my finances, including the money for damage control.

"Oh, he knows," she replied, laughing. "You're paying a pretty penny for this investigator. He's supposedly the best though. Just don't do anything stupid in the meantime to draw more attention to you."

Thoughts of Meghan ran through my mind. "I'm not, but I did meet someone. You'd like her. Her name's Meghan."

"Justin," she scolded. "Getting involved with another woman right now is not good. What if she goes to the press?"

The rain came down harder, and I smiled. "She won't. We promised we'd keep everything a secret. She doesn't want her life exposed to the media."

"What if someone sees you?"

I chuckled. "Not going to happen. She's keeping me busy at her ranch. It'll probably take me all summer just to fix her fence."

Callie gasped. "You're doing manual labor? Wow."

There was grease under my fingernails from working on the truck, but I didn't care. "She needed help, and I wanted to give it to her. I'm telling you, Callie, this girl is something else. I've never met anyone like her."

"That's definitely something, coming from you. What's she like?"

Leaning my head against the barn wall, I closed my eyes and pictured her. "She's beautiful, for starters. She's also an elementary school teacher who can make some killer biscuits. I ate breakfast with her this morning. But most important, she doesn't treat me like I'm a celebrity. When she talks to me, it's like she really wants to get to know who I am."

"She sounds good to me," she murmured. "Just be careful. I know you say you're just friends, but things tend to happen over time. Make sure you think about the repercussions of your actions. Meghan might not be prepared to handle what happens with being involved with a guy like you."

That was what bothered me more than anything. Because of who I was, I'd never be able to have a normal relationship. "I'll figure it out," was all I could say. The rain came down even harder as we said our goodbyes. Meghan and I were just friends. We didn't have to worry about anything, if we kept it all a secret. At least, that was what I was going to tell myself.

CHAPTER NINE

MEGHAN

Justin: Ready for me to come over?

I'D JUST TAKEN THE LAST of the pancakes off the griddle.

Me: Yep! Just fixed breakfast.

Justin: Hell yeah! Be there in a sec.

Me: Just come on in.

It was crazy how easy it was to talk to him. Even with the simple texts, it was like we'd known each other for years. He offered to work on the truck and my fence for free, but I didn't feel right about it, even if he was worth millions. That was why I planned on working with him. If he wasn't going to let me pay him, I'd help him.

The morning was perfect, the smell of last night's rain still in the air. I'd dried off the patio table and set our plate of pancakes and syrup in the middle with two large glasses of orange juice. It wasn't long before I heard the front door open and Justin calling my name.

"Meghan?"

"Out here," I shouted. I could see him through the window, and I waved. He had on his cowboy hat again, wearing jeans and boots with a different plaid shirt from the day before.

When he stepped onto the porch, I got a good look at his clothes, trying my best not to tease him ... only I couldn't help it. "Did you buy a whole new wardrobe just so you'd fit in out here? Never once have I seen a picture of you wearing anything like that."

Pretending to be offended, he slapped a hand over his chest. "Seriously? I wear this shit all the time. Do I look stupid?"

Snickering, I beckoned him over to the table. "Actually, it suits you, but I figured I'd give you a little grief."

He tapped his hat. "I'm enjoying the new look. Might have to wear this kind of stuff when I go back home." His eyes lit up when he noticed our food. "I could get used to this. I don't know what I'm going to do without you when I go back to Charlotte."

I rolled my eyes. "Please. With all the ladies waiting for you back home, I'm sure someone will be dying to cook you breakfast."

He shook his head. "Not like you."

"Yeah, yeah," I teased, grabbing the syrup. I poured it all over my pancakes and dug in. "Breakfast is my favorite meal." Lifting up my plate, I breathed it all in. "Homemade buttermilk pancakes."

I passed the syrup to Justin, and he winked. "Steak is my

favorite. I can kill it on the grill with meats, but other than that, I'm not good around the kitchen."

The pancakes pretty much melted in my mouth. "Seems like we complement each other then," I said, mouth full. "I'm good at everything else besides the grill." Justin tried his best not to smile and failed. Then it hit me what I had done—I'd just talked to him with my mouth full of food. Clearing my throat, I washed my pancakes down with my juice. "Okay, in my defense, I do work with kids all day. I really do have manners."

He snickered and waved me off. "Hey, I'm not saying anything. It's nice to be around a woman who loves to eat." I watched him take a bite of his food and smiled when he moaned in delight. "I don't know what's better, your biscuits or pancakes."

That made me laugh. "Just say they're equal, and I'll be happy. To be honest, I don't know which one I like better either."

His eyes widened. "Oh, I ordered the parts for the truck. They'll be here in a couple of days. Once they come in, I should have it up and running that day."

"Wow, that's awesome. Now you'll have a car to drive around while you're in town." He nodded and continued eating. "Speaking of being in town, when do you have to go back to Charlotte?"

He shrugged. "Early August some time. That's when practices start back up." That was about the time I was headed back to Nags Head to spend the rest of the summer with my family.

"Good. Then we have plenty of time to work on the fence."

"We?" he asked, regarding me curiously.

Nodding, I finished the last bite of my pancakes. "Yep. I'm going to help you since you won't take my money."

By the smile on his face, I knew he wouldn't object. I was

looking forward to spending more time with him. Once he was done with his food, he helped me clean up the table. There were different paint swatches on the kitchen counter, and he held them up.

"What are these for?"

I rinsed off our plates. "For the barn. Which color do you like?"

"None. Why not go with a classic barn red? It's what makes a barn, a barn."

The thought made me laugh. My barn was a faded olive at the moment, and I'd planned on keeping it around the same color. Justin glanced out the back kitchen window and held up the swatches. "You need to go with red. None of these ugly ass green colors," he said, tossing them on the table. He held out his arms. "I'll help you paint it."

Grabbing his arm, I pulled him out the back door, loving the feel of his muscles tensing beneath my touch. "Seriously. You're already doing too much for me as it is. I don't want you spending all your free time here."

"Why not? It's my choice."

Pursing my lips, I glared up at him playfully. "I bet. You just don't want to be alone, and since I'm the only one who knows your secret, you have nobody else."

He smirked. "Damn, you figured me out."

I punched his arm. "Go get my fence done, smartass."

We both laughed, and he followed beside me down to my haggard fence. The fence posts and boards had already been delivered a couple weeks ago, and I had a tub of concrete ready to be mixed. I even had the drills all charged up to help the nailing process go more quickly, but I brought out the hammers and nails instead. It took all I had to contain my smile as Justin studied the old fence.

"All right, let's get started. This shouldn't be too hard." He pointed at the section connected to the barn. "We'll start there and work our way down. Tearing it down should be easy. I can do that myself."

I flourished my hand toward the fence. "Have at it."

He went to work, tearing it down, while I sat in the grass and watched him. He didn't seem to mind, at least not by the sly grins he gave me. "I gave you a break yesterday from asking any questions pertaining to your personal life, but …" I paused, and he froze. His back was to me, so I couldn't see his face.

He'd already torn down one portion of the fence, so I got up and helped him stick in the new fence posts. Grabbing the bucket of freshly mixed concrete, he poured some around them and down into the holes. "What do you want to know?"

"Why did you choose Miranda?" I asked, voice low. Sweat beaded on his forehead, and a look of utter horror passed across his face. I got the impression that he was ashamed.

With a heavy sigh, he stepped back and lowered his gaze. "You asked for honesty, right? And since we're friends, I don't have to worry about you judging me?"

When his head lifted, I could see the seriousness on his face. "I promise," I replied wholeheartedly.

Holding the hammer in his hands, his knuckles turned white from squeezing it so hard. "She was good in bed. That's why she made it so far in the show."

I kind of had a feeling that was one of the reasons, but I'll be damned, it kind of stung to hear him say it. "I really thought the girl you got rid of in week four would've been your choice. I liked her." She was smart and funny, just not over-the-top sexy like most of the other women.

Justin nodded and focused back on the fence. I helped him lift one of the boards to the post, and he nailed them together. "I would've chosen her, but the producers didn't think she was exciting enough."

"More like she didn't cause drama," I interrupted. "She was

a genuinely nice girl." It was obvious she didn't make for exciting TV.

We nailed the last two boards to the posts and that finished up the first section. "She was a very nice girl," he agreed, meeting my gaze. "She almost reminds me of you." That made me smile. While watching the show, I'd thought the same thing. "But unfortunately, I had to let her go. Turns out, Miranda's father had paid off the producers. At the time, I didn't mind, because we were having such a good time together." His jaw clenched and anger flashed in those green eyes of his. "After the show ended—and I was stuck in a year-long engagement—I realized how bad I fucked up. My family and friends hated her just as much as I did." He moved over to the next section of the fence and knocked it down with a sullen kick.

"I'm sorry. It all sounds so complicated." I couldn't imagine having a life like that. It was like something you'd see in the movies.

He scoffed. "You have no idea. Now she's saying I breached our contract by sleeping with five other women. It's all over the tabloids."

"Oh my God," I gasped. "You didn't, did you?"

His eyes blazed. "Do you think I did?"

"You can't blame me for asking, Justin. I only know what I saw of you on television. And frankly, it's not a lot to go on. Just like you don't know me well."

That made his expression soften. "I'm trying to remedy that."

My cheeks burned, and I hoped like hell he didn't notice. "What are you going to do?"

This time, he held the post in place while I poured the concrete. "My brother, Corey, is my agent. He hired a private investigator to get to the bottom of it. As soon as I have the proof I need, I'm going after Miranda and her father."

"Sounds like a huge mess. You're going to have a lot to deal with when you go home."

Sighing, he picked up another board. "You have no idea."

By the end of the afternoon, we were almost finished with six sections of the fence. If we hadn't talked the entire time, we probably could've gotten a lot more done. Covered in sweat, we sat down on the grass, and I tossed him a bottle of water out of the cooler I'd put together after lunch. Storm clouds rolled in overhead, but I didn't want to end the day just yet.

"Hopefully, you got enough of me talking about Miranda today," Justin said, opening up his water.

I guzzled my drink and gasped for air. "More than enough. I don't think I want to hear any more about her."

Justin chuckled. "Sounds good to me. I'd rather talk more about you and your life."

I shrugged. "Not much to tell."

His gaze averted to my phone. "That's not true. I bet you have a ton of pictures that prove otherwise."

Scrolling through my picture gallery, I took a deep breath and handed him my phone. "Fine. Tell me what kind of stories you see."

He took my phone, eyes twinkling as he looked through them. Ever since smart phones became a thing, I'd had all of my pictures transferred to each new phone I'd gotten. That way, I could always have the ones of Trey I'd taken all those years ago.

Justin showed me a photo of Trey and me. "You have a lot to tell, Meghan." It was of us on our wedding day, dancing to our song. "You're very beautiful."

Leaning over his arm, I glanced down at my phone. "Thank you. He was my first love. All he ever wanted to do was help people. It terrified me when he decided to join the military." With a heavy sigh, I closed my eyes. "Even so, I never thought he'd be taken away so soon."

Justin put his arm around my shoulders and squeezed. It shocked me how amazing and comforting it felt. "Does Ellie ever ask about him?" he asked.

A smile lit up my face. "All the time."

He squeezed my shoulder one more time and let go. "Have you dated anyone since your husband?"

"Not really," I answered with a shrug. "Don't get me wrong, I'm more than ready to move on. I just haven't found the right person." He scrolled to a picture of Ellie riding her bike for the first time. "Also, it's a little more complicated when you're a single mother. Some guys don't want everything that comes with that."

Justin smiled at Ellie and chuckled when the next picture popped up, one of her as a toddler after she'd just gotten into my makeup bag. There was lipstick all over her face. "I wish I could meet her. She seems like she'd be fun to be around."

"Oh, she is," I laughed. "I wish you could meet her, too. You both have something in common. For the past two years, she's talked about being an actress when she grows up."

He chuckled. "My kind of girl." Thoughts of them meeting ran through my mind, but it was never going to happen. A part of me wondered if I'd ever see him again once he left town. Justin scrolled through more pictures and then handed me back my phone. "What would you say if we put off working tomorrow and did something fun?"

"What do you have in mind?" I asked. "We can't exactly go out in public."

His grin widened, and he turned to me, pulling out a handful of grass from the ground. "Oh, I know. I was thinking we could go hiking. My land connects to some of the trails in the Grand Teton National Forest, and I thought maybe you'd like to come with me."

Excitement bubbled in my veins. "I'd love to. I'll be at your house first thing in the morning. I have a map of your ranch that the previous owners gave me, showing how to get to all the different trails. Hidden Falls is my absolute favorite."

Justin nodded. "We'll do that one then. And since you're coming over to my place in the morning, I'll fix *you* breakfast." Thunder rumbled in the distance.

"Deal. But it better not be pre-packaged." I was curious to see what he'd cook up.

"Deal," he agreed with a wink. The thunder sounded closer this time, and I felt it vibrate the ground. Justin glanced around and nodded toward the barn just as a flood of rain poured down from the skies. We jumped up and raced for the shelter of the barn, completely drenched.

We both burst out laughing. Raindrops trickled down my face, and I wiped them off, shivering as my shirt stuck to my body. The temperature had cooled off drastically. "That was fast."

Justin had taken off his plaid shirt earlier and set it in the barn. He brought it over to me and turned his back so I could take off my drenched one. "That should help." I slipped out of my wet shirt and put his on. It smelled just like him.

"Thanks. You can turn around now." When he did, I tried not to notice the way his gaze roamed down my body. He'd done that a lot, and each time, it made things inside of me tighten. I wanted him to look at me like that, but I was afraid of getting invested in a relationship when it was obvious nothing could happen between us.

Justin closed the distance and looked down at me, his eyes searching mine. The rain fell down even harder, only adding to the raging tension inside me. "I had fun today, Meghan. Being around you is definitely different from what I'm used to."

"How so?" I murmured, sounding breathless. "Is it because I'm not falling all over you all the time?"

He smirked and moved closer. "Maybe. It does make me question if I'm doing things wrong."

My breath hitched, and I froze. "What do you mean?"

His body brushed up against mine, his gaze on my lips. "All I've wanted to do since I met you was kiss you, but I know I have no right to. We're friends, and I respect that." Closing his eyes, he blew out a frustrated breath. "I know I'm the last person you'd want to get involved with."

"You are," I whispered, "and you're definitely not doing anything wrong. Unfortunately, you're doing it all right." It was like my body moved on its own accord without a single thought from my brain. His eyes snapped open as I slid my hands up his arms. My breath quickened, and my heart felt like it was going to pump out of my chest.

Justin lowered his head, and I lifted up on my toes. The second our lips touched, it was like fire coursing through my body. I couldn't think of anything but the connection between us. I felt vulnerable, but in complete control. There was no right or wrong in our kiss. It was electric, and it felt amazing.

A moan escaped my lips, and Justin held me tighter, pulling me into his body. His tongue caressed mine, and I opened up further. He pushed me back toward the hay bales and covered me with his body. So many emotions ran through me, but I'd never felt so alive in my life. I wanted to embrace it, hold onto it for as long as I could.

Breathing hard, Justin broke from the kiss and rested his forehead to mine. "Fuck, that was intense."

It took all I had to catch my breath. "Tell me about it."

His eyes bored into mine, and he sighed. "As much as I want to keep kissing you, it's probably best we stop. I don't want to get carried away and do something rash."

I could feel the hardness between his legs. "Is it bad that reckless sounds really good right now?"

He chuckled. "Not at all. It's what I want, too. I've always been a live-in-the-now kind of guy, but you can't think like that. Not with your daughter and keeping your life here safe from the media."

The concern on his face only made it harder to think straight. I wanted to live in the now, to throw all reason out the window. I'd never taken a chance on anything. Everything I'd done had always been safe. Clutching his face, I pulled him down to my lips and kissed him gently. "We'll just keep it between us. When you go back home, I'll be here, and you'll go back to your life. This doesn't have to be complicated." The words left my lips, but deep down, I had a feeling it wasn't going to be as easy as that. But I could worry about that later.

Justin carefully slid off of me and helped me up. "You make it sound so simple."

I shrugged. "Is it not?"

A torn expression passed across his face, and it caught me by surprise. He brushed a finger down my cheek, his lips tilting slightly. "I wish it was, Meghan. You have no idea how bad I wish it was."

My phone beeped, and I pulled it out my pocket. It was almost time for my video call with Ellie. Justin nodded toward and smiled. "It's almost time for your date. I should probably go."

I ran a hand down my wet hair. "Probably. Can't have her

seeing us both drenched in the barn. What would I tell my parents?"

"Oh, I know," he teased, lightening the mood. "I'm not parent material." The rain had died down, and he grabbed my hand, pulling me over to the barn entrance. "You know, I don't think I've met anyone's parents other than Miranda's."

I squeezed his hand sympathetically. "If you were a normal guy," I said, "I'd be happy to introduce you to my parents. You're nothing to be ashamed of."

His smile made everything inside of me flutter. "Thanks. Coming from you, at least, I know I'm worthy." He kissed me chastely on the lips. "See you in the morning." Turning on his heel, he strode across the yard. I was about to run to my door when he glanced back at me and waved.

I waved back and leaned against the barn wall. Why was it that the first man to make me feel something was the one guy I couldn't have? I'd spent so many years thinking I was incapable of being attracted to another man. At least I knew I could feel again.

But now I wanted more.

CHAPTER TEN

JUSTIN

All night, I'd thought about that kiss, and came up with one thing ... I wanted her so fucking bad. I'd known it since the day I'd met her, but I'd kept my distance. Unfortunately, my willpower around her was zilch. She wanted me too, which made it even harder. I had to figure out a way to keep her in my life after I left. The only problem was that I came up with nothing.

My phone beeped, drawing me out of my inner turmoil.

Meghan: You awake?

Even just a simple text from her made me feel things I'd never felt before. Grinning wide, I texted her back.

Me: Yup. Just waiting on you. Breakfast is in the oven.

Meghan: Nice. I'll be right there. Just packed up some snacks and waters for us.

I was about to text her back when my phone rang. Corey's name popped up on the screen. "Hey," I said quickly.

"Just checking up on you. How you doing out there?"

"Pretty damn good, actually. Any luck with the investigator?"

Corey sighed. "Not yet. We'll get you out of this mess—don't worry. He'll find something. That's why I was calling. Callie told me she talked to you yesterday and filled you in."

I finished loading my backpack up with enough drinks and snacks for a full day of hiking. "She did. All I know is that when I get back home, it'll be war. I'm not letting that cunt Miranda get away with what she's done."

"Maybe you should come home and deal with it now. The longer you stay gone, the more shit gets started, and you're not here to defend yourself."

"I'm not leaving, Corey." If I left and came back, I'd run the risk of someone recognizing me. If they did, and then saw me with Meghan, it'd ruin everything. The timer went off on the oven so I turned it off and pulled out breakfast.

"What's keeping you there, brother?"

The doorbell rang, and I smiled. "More like someone," I replied.

He sighed. "I had a feeling. Callie told me about Meghan. Hopefully, she knows what she's getting into. She'll be in the middle of this fire when you get back."

That was the last thing I wanted. I'd do anything to keep her away from it. "It's not like that. We're keeping everything a secret."

"You don't sound happy about it."

A part of me wasn't. When the time was right, I wanted to be able to be seen with Meghan in public, but that wasn't what she wanted. "Doesn't matter. It's what she wants," I answered. "We're spending the day hiking."

Corey chuckled. "Have fun with that. I'll call you if anything changes around here."

"Sounds good, bro. Talk soon." We hung up, and I hurried to the door. Meghan waved when I opened the door, greeting me with that sweet smile of hers. She had a backpack strapped to her back, dressed in a long-sleeved, green button-down shirt and denim shorts, and hiking boots. I'd never seen anyone look so sexy in hiking clothes.

"Good morning."

I opened the door, and she walked in, closing her eyes as she breathed in. "I smell sausage."

She followed me into my kitchen, and I showed her the muffin tray, resting on the black marble counter. "They're called Stuffin' Egg Muffins. Basically, it's eggs, cheese, onions, and sausage. My mom used to make them for me all the time."

Picking one out of the pan, she blew off the steam and bit into it, moaning underneath her breath. I loved the sound. "These are so good. We'll have to take some with us."

Chuckling, I grabbed up a muffin and ate it in one bite. "Sounds good to me." I nodded toward her backpack. "Looks like you came prepared."

She pointed over at mine. "Same to you. What all did you pack?"

Grinning slyly, I shrugged. "Drinks and snacks." I didn't want to tell her everything I had in there.

She pulled out the map of my land, and the different trail-heads that connected us. "This is where we have to go," she said, pointing at the Hidden Falls trail. "From the original trailhead at Jenny Lake, it'd be about a ten-mile hike, but from here, it adds on two extra miles."

I shrugged. "You okay with that?"

Rolling her eyes, she scooped up the map. "Please. You're

the one I'm worried about. And speaking of which, you'll need your hat and sunglasses. When we get to the main trail, we'll most definitely be running into other people."

I nodded. "Got it."

I'd thought about that and already had it covered. We finished up breakfast, and it was time to go. She followed me through the house to the back door, her eyes lit with wonderment as she took everything in. "How did you get all the furniture and groceries here without people seeing you?"

I opened the back door and locked it behind us. "Simple. The groceries I had delivered and left on my doorstep, and the furniture was brought in two weeks ago. I paid a team of designers to come in and decorate the place." Now that we were on our way, I slipped on my hat and sunglasses.

"Nice," she said. "If you knew me at that time, I would've done it for you. Interior design was one of my favorite classes in school. Not that I would've done as good of a job as what you have, but it would've been fun to try."

We walked side by side through the field toward the forest. "I hate I didn't know."

Chuckling, Meghan opened up the map. "It's a good thing you didn't. I love horses, so that's probably the theme you'd have." She looked over at me and winked. "And apples. I love my country apple kitchen."

That made me laugh. She did have a ton of apple decorations in her kitchen. "I like your kitchen. It suits you."

I followed her into the forest to what appeared to be a semi-maintained path. It wasn't exactly clear which way we were supposed to go, but that somehow made it more exciting. "Were there any good hiking spots in Minnesota?" she asked.

"Some, but not like this. I used to hike all the time in South Dakota with my brothers. Nothing compares to this, though."

A smile lit up her face. "This is heaven for me." I had to

agree with her. I'd never felt so at peace in a place before. The stream that connected to my lake bubbled up ahead. I could hear the roaring water as it cascaded down the various rocks. We stopped at the small bridge, and I pulled out my phone. I took a picture of her as she stared at the water.

Her head jerked my way, and she glanced down at my phone. "You better not share that on your social media. I'll deny ever knowing you."

I laughed. "Would you really?"

She winked. "Oh yeah. That's the real reason why I want this to be a secret." Her lips pulled back slyly. "I'm embarrassed of you. Who in their right mind would want to be seen with a celebrity?" Pulling out her phone, she took pictures of the stream, and then turned to me, grinning wide as she snapped ones of me. "When you're gone, I'll need something to remember you by."

The words stung, and even as she said it, I could tell it bothered her too. Even though we'd only spent a few days together, I couldn't imagine never seeing her again. She turned to walk away, but I grabbed her hand and pulled her back.

"What if I didn't have all the baggage looming over me? What if I was just a normal guy, would you want to be with someone like me?" I had to believe there was someone out there who could see past all my flaws, and that I wasn't just an arrogant celebrity who only cared about the conquest. It was rare to find genuine people like that in my world.

Meghan looked right in my eyes and sighed. "But your life isn't normal, Justin."

I pulled her into me, holding her close. Her body melted into mine, and it was the answer I needed. "What if it was?" I murmured. "I know I'm not the only one who feels something here."

Lifting a hand, she placed it on my cheek. I wanted to kiss

her again like I did the night before. Hell, I wanted much more than that. "You're a good guy, and I see it in your eyes. The things I feel are so foreign to me right now. I haven't had these kinds of feelings in a long time."

I placed my hand over hers and kissed her palm. "Is that good or bad?" Her breath hitched, and I made my move.

I lowered my lips to hers, and she moaned. She tasted like sweet strawberries. "Definitely good." She rested her head against my chest and snickered. It was obvious she could feel a certain appendage that was happy to rub against her. "You're killing me, Justin. I can't think straight when you do things like that."

Chuckling, I let her go, and we continued through the woods. "Can't help it. I've been thinking about that kiss since last night. Not to mention, you're sexy as hell. It's hard for me not to get excited." I reached out and held her hand.

It took all the willpower I had not to take her in the barn the night before. Everything felt right, but intellectually I knew it wasn't the right time or place. If we ever did take that step, it needed to be special. Meghan deserved it to be.

"Tell me about your horse," I called out. I needed something to deter my mind away from kisses in the barn.

Brows furrowed, she glanced over at me. "The one I had to sell?" I nodded, and a sad smile spread across her face. "His name was Firefly. He was chocolate-colored with a white main and tail." She closed her eyes as if she could see him in her mind. "He also had white markings on his body. When he wasn't wearing a saddle, it looked like a huge heart."

"Who did you sell him to?" I wondered.

She sighed. "To Danny Wilford, the principal of my school. He knew I needed the money, so he bought him from me. I go out there from time to time to see him. Danny boards and takes care of horses as a side job."

That was good to know. For the next couple of hours, we

made it through my land to the main trailhead. We spent some of it talking, but the rest was in silence. Just being around her was enough for me.

So far, we hadn't run into anyone, but I heard a few voices further up the trail. Meghan did too and turned to me, slowly letting my hand go. "If anyone tries to talk to us, let me handle it. We don't want anyone recognizing you."

My lips pulled back. "I've trained to be an actor all my life, sweetheart. You wouldn't believe how many voices I can do."

That piqued her interest. Crossing her arms over chest, she leaned against a tree. "Go ahead, then. Enlighten me."

I'd studied all sorts of accents for years. I could do an amazing Australian one. In fact, it was my favorite. Clearing my throat, I sidled up to her and pressed my body against hers. "How about this one? You could pretend I'm your lover from Australia who's here for a visit." Her eyes widened, and I moved back. "Or I can be your cousin. It's whatever you prefer."

Grabbing her chest, she stared at me as if she'd never seen me before. "Oh my God, you sound just like Chris Hemsworth. You even kind of look like him, too, with the blond hair." She glanced around quickly. "Do me a favor and do a Southern accent from North Carolina if someone talks to you. Can't have you drawing *more* attention to yourself."

She fanned herself and I smiled. "Afraid I might get other women's attention?"

Rolling her eyes, she pushed me away. "Don't get a big head on me now."

The voices sounded closer, and I could see the two men approaching us. Meghan froze and blew out a nervous breath. "Oh, shit. I know them. Grant's one of my friends, and that's his boyfriend, Cameron. I graduated with Grant."

"What's the problem then?" I asked curiously.

"I never called him to let him know I was back in town.

He's my hiking buddy. I've been so distracted with you that I've neglected him."

Chuckling, I bumped her with my shoulder. "You're a bad friend."

Grant and Cameron were so busy in conversation that it took a while for them to realize we were right in their path. When Grant noticed Meghan, his eyes lit up, and he held out his arms. He had floppy dark hair, and his shorts were a little snug. It wasn't until he spoke when it all became apparent. "Girl, what are you doing here?" His voice was very feminine and high-pitched.

Meghan rushed up to him and squeezed him, then wrapped her arms around his companion. "My nephew was supposed to work on my fence this summer, but he got the chance to study abroad. I came home to find someone else."

Grant rested his hands on his hips. "And you failed to let me know you were back in town? Where's Ellie?"

She clutched his arm. "I'm so sorry about that. Ellie's still in Nags Head with my family. I've been so busy since I came back."

Grant's focus landed on me. "I see that. Who's your friend?"

I held out my hand, giving my best Southern accent. "Justin. I'm Meghan's cousin from Tennessee."

Meghan tried her best not to laugh and ended up looking away from me. The accent sounded ridiculous coming from my mouth. I might've laid it on a little too thick. Grant shook my hand. "It's nice to meet you, Justin. I'm Grant, and this is my boyfriend, Cameron." I shook Cameron's hand and smiled at them both. Grant turned to Meghan and hugged her again. "Now that you're back, we need to get together for dinner."

"Definitely," Meghan replied. "I'll call you."

Grant nodded at me, and they started on their way. "Talk to you soon."

Once they were out of ear shot, Meghan burst out laughing and grabbed my arm. "That was too funny. You sounded so country."

I beamed. "What can I say? I'm a natural."

Over the next hour or so, we bypassed a couple other hikers as they walked down the trail, but none of them paid attention to us. A bridge lay up ahead, and I could hear the massive waterfall in the distance. Meghan bounced on her feet and pointed toward the sound. "We're almost there. You're going to love it."

We crossed over the bridge and hiked up the hill. The waterfall got louder, and when we reached the top, there it was. It was massive. Sprays of water hit us from where we stood, and it felt amazing. Meghan held out her arms with the biggest smile on her face. "So … what do you think? Was it worth the hike?"

I pulled out my phone and took her picture. "You have no idea."

CHAPTER ELEVEN

MEGHAN

No matter how many times I hiked to Hidden Falls, it never got old. I could sit and stare at the waterfall for hours, and that's just what Justin and I did. We had the place all to ourselves. There was a huge boulder I always rested on when visiting, so we had our picnic on top of it and spent the rest of the time lying in the sun.

"What made you want to be a teacher?" he asked.

I looked over at him, and he was leaned up on his elbow, staring at me. I turned my body toward him and mirrored his stance. "I love kids, and I love teaching. It runs in my family. Both my mom and my sister are teachers, but my mom retired a few years ago."

His smile faded. "Did you and Trey want a big family?"

My chest tightened, and I fought back the burn behind my eyes. "We did. The plan was that Trey was going to go on that last mission and be done. What about you?" I asked, changing the subject. "I bet you wanted to have a dozen kids with Miranda."

He burst out laughing and leaned back on the rock. "Are you kidding? I wanted to have a hundred." I laughed along with him until he stopped and turned back to me. He stared at me and took a deep breath, his expression serious. "Want to know something?"

"Of course," I said, sliding closer to him.

He took another deep breath and released it slowly. "Before I came out here, a harsh realization pretty much smacked me across the face."

"What?" I'd never seen him look so vulnerable. It was almost as if he was a different person. Or maybe he was just letting me see a whole new part of him that the world didn't know.

His attention averted to the waterfall. "After we won the Stanley Cup, our team had a celebration party. It hit me that all of my friends and family were on a different level than me. They were happy. My sister's married to one of my teammates and pregnant with his baby. My oldest brother, Brant, is married with a family. Corey is engaged to my sister's best friend. And my cousin, Maddox, just had a baby with his wife."

Little did he know that I had the same feelings. Yes, I was married eight years ago, but it was only for two glorious months. Trey was overseas for a month of it. "You're not the only one who thinks that way, Justin." His eyes met mine, and he looked surprised. "All of my friends are happily married or in serious relationships right now. I'm thirty years old. I should be that way too, and I'm not."

"Do you want to be?" he asked.

"Who doesn't? It's only natural. You can only be the sexy bachelor for so long before you want more. Just like I don't want to be a single mother forever. I love my daughter more than anything, and she makes me happy, but there are times I just feel ... alone."

He sat up and pulled me with him. "Looks like we have more in common than we thought."

Butterflies fluttered in my stomach, and I wanted them to go away, but they kept coming back with a vengeance every time Justin said something that pulled at my heart. Even when he kissed me, I wanted more. I needed to keep my wits about me, but it was so hard. Being around him made me want things I couldn't have with him. Yes, I could for the time being, but could I honestly forget about him when he left? No. Was it a risk I was willing to take? My body said yes, but my mind said no.

I looked up at the sky and my heart raced. Time had gone by way too quickly. Pulling out my phone, I gasped when I saw what time it was. "Holy shit, we have to go. It's getting late." I jumped up, and Justin handed me my bag.

He glanced down at his phone. "Think we can make it back before dark?"

"I sure as hell hope so." Justin jumped down off the boulder and helped me off. I took one last look at the waterfall, and we were on our way. "I can't believe we lost track of time."

Justin chuckled. "Time flies when you're having fun. At least we have tons of food if we get stuck out here overnight."

I picked up my pace. "As long as the bears don't come after us. It's a good thing I always carry bear spray and a gun when I hike." I'd heard so many stories of bear attacks, and I didn't want to be another statistic. Ellie was often with me, and I wanted to make sure we were protected as much as could be.

Justin opened his bag and pulled out his own can of bear spray. "I came prepared too."

"Nice. I'm impressed."

He shrugged. "I'm smart when I want to be." The sky had

started to dim, and with us being beneath the canopy of the trees, it appeared even darker. I could see our crossroads up ahead, right across from the two big boulders that looked two giant butt cheeks. Justin pointed at it. "That's where we turn off, right?"

I nodded. "Yep. Now we'll need the map." I grabbed it out of my bag, and we continued on our way. "Speaking of being smart, why didn't you ever go to college?"

Justin followed along behind me since the trail had narrowed. I glanced back at him and he shrugged. "School was never really my thing. I did take some acting classes. Hockey is my life right now. I'd hoped to be able to transition to acting after I retired, but I doubt that'll happen now. Miranda's father has too many ties in Hollywood."

I stopped and faced him. "Then you make it happen. Karma's a bitch, and I have no doubt Miranda's going to get her comeuppance, but *you* have to go after what you want. If you want to be in movies after you retire, then do it. She can't stop you."

Grinning devilishly, he closed the distance between us. "You have that kind of faith in me?"

I lifted up on my toes and kissed him gently. "Of course. I've seen you on the ice, Justin Davis. You don't take me as the kind of guy to give in or let anyone stop you, even if they do have a reputation."

Justin smiled down at me. "I wish I'd known you before."

Taking his hand, I pulled him through the woods. "At least you know me now." Panic settled in my gut. It was getting late, and there was no way we could get through the woods in the dark. We had another mile and a half, but without adequate lighting, I could easily get us lost. Heart racing, I stopped and looked around. "I hate to say this, but I think we're screwed." There was a small clearing beside the stream, but there was no shelter. It was a good thing it was summertime. The night temperatures could get down into the thirties, even in June, but I prayed that wasn't the case tonight.

Justin dropped his bag to the ground and pulled out a flashlight. "We'll be fine."

I shook my head. "I'm not navigating through the forest with just a flashlight."

"I wasn't saying we should," he said, winking at me. "Maybe we should camp out, to be on the safe side."

"Have you lost your mind?" I flourished my hand around us. "We can't sleep out here in the open. You do realize there are a shit-ton of bears and what not out here, right?"

He shrugged. "You have your gun and we both have bear spray."

I looked at him like he'd lost his mind; he was insane. Plus, it was almost time for Ellie to video call me, and I wasn't alone at home. I peered around at our surroundings and found a tree that had fallen over. Right on time, my phone started to ring. Justin dropped his bag to the ground and started rummaging through it.

"Hey," I called out. He smiled up at me, and it was like every fear vanished. "Ellie's calling me, so mum's the word."

Hands in the air, he sat down on the ground. "Not a peep."

I swiped a finger across my phone and Ellie appeared, her hair in curls down her back. "Look at you," I gushed. "Is Maw Maw and Paw Paw taking you out tonight?"

She nodded. "We're going to eat steak. Paw Paw said I could get dessert if I eat all my food."

My stomach growled, and all I could think about was how my dinner was going to be leftovers from our picnic. "That sounds yummy, Ellie-Bear. I can't wait to come back out there."

Her lower lip trembled slightly. "I miss you, Mommy. Is the fence getting done?"

My eyes burned, and I could tell that Justin was watching

me. "Almost. There's still a lot left. At least, when you come back home, it'll be finished, and so will the barn. You'll be surprised."

In the background, my mother appeared and waved. "Hey, baby. What are you doing out in the woods?"

Ellie's eyes narrowed as if she just realized it. "Yeah, Mommy. Why are you out there?"

I shrugged, trying my best to think up something off the top of my head. "Thought I saw a baby deer. I didn't want it to be alone without its mother." I looked around as if searching for it. "But I can't see it anymore."

My mother waved again. "It was good seeing you, honey." She squeezed Ellie's shoulders. "It's time for us to go, before the restaurant gets crowded."

I blew a kiss to Ellie. "Sweet dreams tonight, baby girl. I'll talk to you tomorrow. I love you."

She blew a kiss back. "I love you too." As always, I waited for her to hang up first. If it was up to me, I'd never be able to do it.

"She sounds so sweet," Justin said, smiling sadly at me. "I can tell you miss her."

My chest tightened. "I do."

Rummaging through his bag again, he pulled out a black pouch. "I'll work extra hard to get the fence and barn done so you can get back to her." I was dying to see her and hold her in my arms again, but the second I left, I'd never see him again. A part of me felt guilty for wanting that extra time with him when I knew I'd never have it again once my life went back to normal.

"What's that?" I asked, nodding at the pouch.

A smug smile spread across his face. "While you were freaking out about us being stuck out here, you failed to let me elaborate on how prepared I was." He opened the pouch, and out popped one of those ready-made tents. Surprisingly enough it was moderately sized and could probably fit four people. The top had a mesh area where you could see out. There was a whole area of soft, green grass by the stream, and he set it there.

Mouth gaping, I walked over to it and looked inside. "I'm really impressed now."

He searched through his bag again and pulled out a blanket. "We won't freeze, either." Before crawling inside, I took off my boots and set them outside the tent. Justin did the same and climbed in with me. "The flashlight has fresh batteries, so we should be good there too."

Once inside, Justin zipped us up, and I lay down with my hands behind my neck. All I could see through the mesh top were the trees and a small amount of sky that would soon be pitch black. Now that we weren't moving on the trail, the cold had started to register. Even if it was officially summer, the nighttime temperatures dropped drastically from the days.

Justin wrapped the blanket around us and pulled me into his arms. It felt good lying against his chest and hearing his heart beat. "This isn't so bad, is it?"

I rolled my eyes. "Actually, no. But it would've been if we didn't have the tent."

His fingers brushed across my neck to move my hair away. "I had fun today. Then again, every day with you has been exactly what I needed."

He placed a hand over mine, and I squeezed it. "If you want to take tomorrow off from the fence, that's fine. I don't want you feeling like you have to work on it every day. You have a life besides helping me out."

Leaning his body away, he lowered me down to my back and rested on his side next me, his head propped on his hand as he looked down at me. "There's nowhere else I want to be."

The way he looked at me, with those green eyes full of raw passion, I couldn't help but wonder how many women he'd looked at the same way. I wanted to believe I was special, that what we were doing was something completely different than what he'd ever done with anyone else.

"How many women have you been in love with?" I asked, murmuring the words.

A sigh escaped his lips and he moved closer. The warmth of his body seeped into mine, and I shivered. I wanted him closer. "To be honest, I don't know if I ever have been." He traced my lips with his thumb. "The way I feel when I'm around you is stronger than anything I've ever felt with anyone else."

Heart racing, I knew exactly how he felt. "Why is that, you think?"

His gaze drifted to my lips, but then slowly moved back to my eyes. "I have a theory, but I don't think you're ready to hear it." My stomach fluttered, and a part of me wanted desperately to hear him say he was falling for me, but I didn't want to get my hopes up. In the end, it'd only hurt me more. There could never be anything serious between us. I opened my mouth to speak, but he pressed his finger to my lips. "Let's not get into that right now. I have a question for *you.*"

"What?" I whispered.

"How many men have you been in love with?"

A number popped into my head, but I stored it away. It was too soon to feel like that for him … or was it? Why did people want what they couldn't have? "One," I answered. "It was a good love, too, while it lasted."

Justin nodded, clearly understanding I was referring to my late husband. "Was he the only man you'd ever been intimate with?"

"Yes," I replied. "I'd never had anyone spark that kind of interest in me after he died. Well, except for …"

His eyes flashed, and it made everything inside of me tighten. He moved closer and slid his hands over my stomach.

"Except for who?" he said, brushing his stubbly cheek against my neck. The second his warm lips touched my skin, my eyes rolled back into my head. Chill bumps fanned out across my body, and my breath hitched.

"You already know."

Ever so gently, he rolled on top of me and settled between my legs. His hips moved against mine, and a moan escaped my lips. He smiled and kissed me harder, earning another strangled moan. "I like the sound of that."

"Unfortunately, there's something we need to talk about."

His lips stilled against mine, and he lifted up on his elbows. With a sigh, he nodded. "You want to know if I'm safe."

He stared right into my eyes, and I blew out a nervous breath. "I do. Surely, you know why." There was no telling how many women he'd been with. I didn't want to think about it, but I had to protect myself.

A sad expression passed across his face. "I was tested for everything under the sun a few months back. I haven't been with anyone since. But if you want to wait until I can show you proof, we can."

Relief washed through me. Taking his face in my hands, I pulled him closer. "I trust you, Justin. And since we're on this kind of subject, you should know I'm protected as well. I've been on the pill for years." Not that I needed protection from pregnancy. It was to keep me regular.

Justin grinned wide. "I like the sound of that even better." His lips descended on me again, and he pushed his hips against mine, even more feverishly than before. I thought I was going to lose my mind.

My body was on fire. Every single place he touched felt like I was going to explode. Resting my hands on his chest, I pushed him gently. He sat up and looked down at me, his arms caging me in. "It's been a long time since I've done this, Justin."

Understanding flashed across his face, and he nodded. "I know. Believe it or not, it's been a while for me too. That's why I plan to go slow, for both our sakes. I don't want to hurt you. If you want me to stop, I'll move right over to my side of the tent."

I shook my head, body trembling with anticipation. "No. I want this. I want you. It's just ..."

His brows furrowed. "It's just what?"

As much as I felt confident with myself and my body, I wasn't a model or a movie star. My body wasn't perfect. I had flaws. It came with having a baby, and I was so scared for him to see them.

Justin clasped my face, his concerned gaze on mine. "It's just what, Meghan? Tell me."

His eyes bored into mine, and I had to look away; it was too intense. "I don't have the kind of body you're used to seeing," I whispered. "I'm not as sexy as the women you've been with. I have stretch marks on my stomach, and my breasts aren't as perky as they used to be."

"Seriously?" He grabbed my chin and pulled me back. "You have no idea how fucking sexy you are. I don't care what kind of marks you have on your body." A tear fell down my cheek, and he wiped it away. "When I say you're beautiful, it means every single part of you."

"Promise?"

He nodded. "I promise. No amount of flaws you think you might have could ever stop me from being with you tonight."

His lips closed over mine, slowly at first, but then it grew urgent. The second his hand slipped up my shirt to massage my breast, I was done. I wanted more ... a lot more. "More," I begged.

His eyes sparked, then he lifted my shirt and unclasped my bra, freeing my aching breasts. I gasped when he closed his lips over my nipple, sucking it between his teeth. I grabbed onto his shoulders, and everything inside of me tightened. I wrapped my legs around his waist and worked myself over his erection.

"Ah fuck," he moaned. He unlatched my legs and kept his gaze on mine as he unbuttoned my shorts and pulled them off, along with my underwear. I kicked them aside, and he slid his fingers between my legs. My eyes rolled into the back of my head as he pushed one inside, then another.

He pulled them out and stared down at me when he put them in his mouth. The level of raw intensity in his gaze made me tremble. I'd never had anyone look at me like that before. My breaths came out quick, my heart thumping in my chest. The anticipation was torture.

Grabbing the waistband of his jeans, I tugged them as hard as I could. "These need to come off now." Chuckling, he peeled them off, and I helped him with his shirt. It was as if we were both starved for each other. His kisses were wild, all over my body, and I felt like at any moment, I'd go insane from his touch.

Justin brushed the hair away from my face, his arousal aligning with my opening. When he pushed himself inside, I cried out and dug my nails into his back, relishing the feel of him stretching me wide. It took a few seconds to get used to him, but when I did, I wrapped my legs around his waist, squeezing as he pushed inside of me. His thrusts grew hard and fast. I was so close to the edge, I was about to explode.

He trailed his lips to my neck and bit down, his fingers digging in to my hips. "You feel so fucking good."

I rocked my hips against his and cried out as my release exploded through every nerve in my body. Justin followed closely behind, grunting as his cock pulsated inside me. My whole body trembled, and I ached for more.

Still connected, he rested on his elbows and gazed down at me. "You okay? At first, I thought maybe I hurt you."

I shook my head. “It was a good hurt.”

He kissed me and rested his forehead to mine. “I’m sorry it went so fast. I wasn’t lying when I said it’d been a while for me too.”

A giggle escaped my lips. “Don’t worry. We have plenty of time to build up your stamina.”

Waggling his eyebrows, he smiled down at me. “And we can start tonight.”

CHAPTER TWLEVE

JUSTIN

The night had been so fucking amazing. We woke up to the sun shining down into the tent. Luckily, there were no run-ins with bears or any other animals in the middle of the night. The sounds we made probably kept them away. I couldn't remember the last time I'd been with a woman that I couldn't get enough of. We'd slept until mid-morning, and I'd held her in my arms the entire time. Her hair was a mess, but she was still the most beautiful woman I'd ever seen. I looked over at her and smiled. We were almost back to my ranch.

"What?" she said, returning my smile.

I shrugged. "Just thinking how sexy you are this morning."

Rolling her eyes, she tried to run a hand through her hair, and her fingers got caught. "Yeah, right. I'm ready to get home and take a shower." Her stomach growled, and I could hear it. "And I'm starving."

Laughing, I grabbed my stomach. "So am I. How about I

walk you home and then I grab some clothes and stay at your house tonight?"

She bit her lip and tried her best not to smile. "Are you not tired of me after last night?"

I clutched her around the waist and she squealed. "Hell no. Not even close. You can't get rid of me that easily."

It was so easy to live in the moment, but the nagging realization that it was only temporary loomed in the back of my mind. I refused to listen to it. She belonged in Wyoming, and I belonged in Charlotte. I wanted to find a way around that but came up empty. Still, I wasn't ready to let her go.

My ranch came into view, and we walked across the field past the side of my house. She looked at me like I'd lost my mind. "What are you doing?"

I pointed at the road. "Walking you home. What kind of gentleman would I be if I didn't."

She clutched my arm and winked. "You just want to make sure there's no one at my house waiting for me."

"What can I say? You're mine ... at least, for the time being."

I was hoping to get a reaction from her, but she said nothing. It was the first time I'd ever wanted something more than sex from someone. I wasn't the type to sit back and let things play out, but with Meghan, I wasn't sure I had a choice.

We walked the rest of the way in silence, and I stopped at her door. She wrapped her arms around my neck, and I held her tight. "After I take a shower, I'll fix us something to eat."

"Then we can work on the fence," I added.

Her eyes twinkled. "And maybe we can do a few other things as well."

The woman was going to kill me. I leaned down and kissed her, loving the way she opened up to me. "I'll be back."

"Okay," she murmured.

Turning on my heel, I headed down her long driveway. My

phone was almost dead, but I had enough to make a call. When it came to women, I was so fucking lost. I never cared before now. The phone rang and rang, and I was prepared to leave Callie a message, but she answered.

"Hey."

"Hey, sis. I was going to leave you a message. Thought you'd be at work by now."

She sighed. "I would be under normal circumstances, but this pregnancy is kicking my butt. Dallas is insisting I take time off until after the baby's born. And you know him. It was either I request it off, or he was going to demand it."

Chuckling, I shook my head. That was Dallas Easton for you. He was our hotheaded goalie. However, when it came to my sister, I expected nothing less from him. "You married him," I teased.

"I heard that!" Dallas shouted in the background.

Callie snickered and shouted back. "I didn't realize someone was eavesdropping. Let me get you off of speaker-phone so my caveman of a husband can't hear us."

I loved hearing their banters. It was always like that between them two. The first time they officially met was on the ice, when Callie was in full body hockey gear. She grew up playing with Maddox and me. That day, Dallas had no clue she was a female. It pissed him off that she'd gotten several pucks past him into the goal. However, when he found out she was a woman, that was it; he fell in love with her. I was beginning to think I knew what it was like to fall that hard.

"Okay, you're off speakerphone now. Is everything okay?"

I came to the top of road and crossed over to my land. "Everything's great, actually. Yesterday was literally one of the best days I've had in a long time."

"Then why don't you sound happy about that?"

With a heavy sigh, I walked over to my fence and leaned against it. My land was something you'd see on a post card. I never thought I'd feel so close to it. "I really love it here, Callie. I know I haven't been here long, but it's starting to feel like home."

"This girl has really done a number on you," she said, sounding unsure.

Groaning, I ran a hand through my hair and continued toward my ranch. "You have no idea. I've been with her every single day and we work so effortlessly together. It's a different world out here."

"Are you falling for her?"

My chest tightened. There were so many things I wanted to tell Meghan, but I couldn't. It was best I kept it all to myself. "I am," I confessed. "When we were together last night, there was no denying the connection we have. I've never felt that with anyone."

A soft laugh escaped her lips. "The day finally came. My brother's in love." She giggled again. "So when do I get to meet her?"

"You don't."

"What? Why not?"

And this was where all the complications reared their ugly heads. "Believe me, I want you to meet her, but it's not my choice. Meghan doesn't want the media attention." I cleared my throat. "There are some things you don't know about her. It's not only herself she's protecting."

She gasped. "Oh my God, she's not married, is she?"

Pulling out my keys, I unlocked the front door of my cabin and walked inside. "She was. He died eight years ago in Afghanistan."

"Oh no, how awful."

I tossed my keys on the kitchen counter and sat down at my table. "Yep. I'm the first man she's been with since he passed away."

"Is that it?" she asked.

Blowing out a heavy breath, I closed my eyes. Once I told her the rest, I knew what she'd say about it. I just wasn't ready to hear it. "No," I replied reluctantly. "There's something else." I waited a few more seconds. "She has a daughter ... Ellie."

The line went silent, and I could hear her suck in a breath. "Wow. I was not expecting that one."

"I haven't met her yet. She's in the Outer Banks with Meghan's parents for the summer."

"Guess I can see why she wants to stay out of the media, especially with all the shit from Miranda right now. She probably doesn't want herself or Ellie to be in the middle of it."

I didn't want to bring any hardship to them, but I knew I'd do everything in my power to protect them. I wanted to tell Meghan that, but I didn't want to see the doubt on her face. "Even when I get all of that handled, it's not going to matter. Meghan doesn't want to be a part of that world."

"What if you told her how you truly feel? Don't you think she might change her mind?"

I shook my head. "It won't matter. In a few weeks, she's leaving to go back to Nags Head to get her daughter, and I'm coming back to Charlotte. It'll all be over. She belongs here, and I belong there."

She sniffled, and I froze. "You okay?"

"Yeah. I think these pregnancy hormones are making me crazy. You sound so sad, and it breaks my heart. Is there anything I can do?"

I stood and walked over to the window where I could see Meghan's home. "No. I'm just going to enjoy the time I have left with her. I have to respect her decision." Even though it killed me inside.

CHAPTER THIRTEEN

MEGHAN

I couldn't remember the last time I'd danced around in the shower with a smile on my face. I was so incredibly happy—it felt like I could do anything. I threw on a clean pair of shorts and tank top and wrapped my wet hair into a bun. Justin and I were probably going to work on the fence all day, so there was no reason to fix it.

Stomach growling, I danced my way into the kitchen, humming my favorite Charlie Puth song. My phone was dead on the counter, so I plugged it in and got started on cooking breakfast. The smell of bacon filled the air, and I hoped like hell Justin was almost to my house. If not, I was going to eat without him.

Grinning wide, I checked the charge on my phone and sent him a text.

Me: Breakfast is almost done. I'm going to eat without you. 😊

My phone beeped, and I thought it was going to be a silly reply, but it wasn't him. There were three missed calls from Samantha and a couple of texts from her asking where I was. "Shit," I groaned, fumbling to call her back.

"Don't worry," a voice called out. "I know you're still alive."

I jerked around and there Samantha was, her arms crossed over her chest. Blonde hair pulled high in a ponytail, she had on a pair of denim shorts and a pink tank top. It was obvious she didn't have to work. The curious smile on her face only added to my nervousness. "Sam, what are you doing here?"

Gaze narrowed humorously, she pursed her lips. "If you'd have returned my calls, I wouldn't have had to come by. I was worried about you. From what I can tell, it seems like you're doing pretty well." She leaned against the kitchen counter and studied me. "More than pretty well. You're positively glowing. Who is he?"

"He? I have no clue what you're talking about." I waved her off and finished scrambling the eggs, making sure to keep my back to her. She'd see the truth on my face.

"You can't lie to me, Meg," she said, laughing. "Emmett already said he heard you talking to someone out back the other day. Why are you trying to hide this guy?" She squeezed my shoulder gently. "If you're worried about what Emmett will say, you have nothing to worry about. He's ready for you to move on." If she only knew.

"I'm not hiding anyone," I lied.

She glanced over my shoulder at all the food I'd made. "Looks good. It's way more than you'll eat. Almost like you were cooking for two, and you obviously didn't know I was stopping by."

"Geez, you're annoying me." Laughing, I grabbed two

plates out of the cabinet and handed her one. "Get some if you're hungry. I guess I went a little overboard." By the look on her face, she didn't believe me. She scooped some eggs onto her plate and picked up a piece of bacon and a slice of toast. "Do you not have to work today?"

She took her plate and sat down at the table. "Nope. I worked a double shift and took today off to catch a break. Thought I'd hang out with you since I haven't seen you in a while." She watched me like a hawk as I fixed my plate of food. I wanted to text Justin to tell him not to come over, but then she'd ask who I was texting. It was so hard to lie to someone who'd been my best friend for most of my life. Luckily, Justin would see her car in the driveway and know to stay away.

Pulse racing, I grabbed my plate and sat down at the table with her. I didn't know what to say. I hated keeping secrets from her, but I knew without a doubt that if Emmett were to find out about Justin, he'd strongly disapprove simply because of who he was.

"Do you want something to drink?" I asked, trying to get away from her unrelenting stare.

She smiled wide. "Sure. Thanks."

I got up and fetched the orange juice out of the refrigerator. When I opened the cabinet to grab some cups, it was when I noticed the driveway. "Where's your car?" I asked, the words sounding desperate as they came out of my mouth.

Samantha nodded toward the back of the house. "I brought the four-wheeler. It was the quickest way to get here to make sure you were okay."

Throwing my hands in the air, I huffed. "If I don't answer the phone right when you call, it doesn't mean there's something wrong."

Her gaze saddened. "I know, Meg. It's just you've always answered me. I was worried." She looked down at her plate. "I always worry about you. Trey's been gone for eight years, and you haven't moved on." A tear fell down her cheek. "I want you to move on."

Footsteps echoed off the front porch, and I sucked in a breath. Frozen in place, I stared at the door as Justin knocked and came right on in. "Knock, knock," he called out. He stopped mid-step the second he noticed Samantha.

She dropped her fork on her plate, and eggs splattered everywhere. "Oh my God. You're ..." Hands shaking, she stood and stumbled back to me, keeping her eyes on him. "He's ..."

Sighing, I put my arm around her shoulders. "Samantha, this is Justin. The guy I've been seeing."

SAMANTHA'S REACTION TO SEEING JUSTIN was pretty much the way I imagined every female to do in his presence. She stumbled over her words until I had to make her go outside to get some fresh air. For the past thirty minutes, all she'd done was sit at my patio table and stare at Justin while he worked on the fence and then over at me with a complete look of shock on her face. I felt bad for not helping him, but he knew I needed to deal with Samantha.

"Are you going to say something or just stare at us all day?" I asked her.

She sipped her orange juice and set it down on the table. Justin glanced over at us and smiled reassuringly. I was glad he stayed. I didn't know how he was going to react. Samantha shook her head and focused on me.

"How? I'm so confused right now."

My gaze instantly found Justin. It was like anytime he was around, I couldn't look at anything else. "I gave him a ride home from the airport. Turns out, he bought the Southfork Ranch from the McEntire's." I closed my eyes and replayed our first meeting in my head.

"Did you not go crazy when you met him?" she asked incredulously.

I shook my head and laughed. "Nope. That's just you. I actually pretended not to know him. It was fun at first, but then I came clean and told him I knew. We both promised to keep his whereabouts a secret. I don't want the media knowing he's here, much less involved with me. I have Ellie to protect."

Her eyes widened, and she grabbed my hands. "Are you sleeping with him?" My cheeks burned, and I bit my lip. "Holy shit, you are. This is insane. The guy's a celebrity, and he's out here fixing your fence."

I pointed to Trey's blue truck. "And the truck. Once the parts are in, he's going to get it running again. I told him he could have it if he got it fixed."

"Wow," she gasped, letting my hands go. "You really have moved on. Never thought you'd get rid of it."

I shrugged. "It's time. I'm pretty sure he'll leave it here when he goes back to Charlotte. He only has a few weeks left before hockey starts up."

Her brows furrowed. "What about you? What are you going to do?"

She finished off her juice, and I grabbed her cup to take it inside. I walked over to the edge of my patio and watched Justin. "What can I do, Sam? We only have a few weeks together before we go back to our normal lives. Am I going to miss him?" I glanced at her over my shoulder. "Yes, I am. The man makes me feel more alive than I've felt in a long time. I don't want it to end, but there's no other choice." Eyes burning, I hurried inside and set her cup in the sink. I didn't realize she was behind me until she hugged me.

"You could always have both, Meghan. There are no rules when it comes to love. The guy does have some baggage right now, so I can see why you don't want anyone knowing, but don't let that scare you away."

I really wanted to believe her, but it wasn't going to be that easy. I patted her hands and turned around, hoping she couldn't see my insecurities. I had to believe I was doing the right thing. "It's for the best. In a few weeks, he'll go his way, and I'll go mine. I'm fine with it. Ellie doesn't have to know and neither does Emmett. It'll be our secret."

Her lips tilted slightly, and she shook her head, clearly not believing me. "Keep telling yourself that, babe. I don't want to see you get hurt."

"You won't," I said, brightening my smile. "Now that you're calmed down, let's introduce you to him. I don't want him thinking my best friend is a starstruck idiot."

She took a deep breath and let it out slow. "Okay, I can do this."

She followed me outside, and I tried not to laugh. Her hands were shaking from being so nervous. Justin had already finished a whole two sections of fence by himself. I cleared my throat, and he turned around, showing off his glorious abs. The smile he gave Samantha made her sway on her feet. It was a good thing Emmett wasn't there.

"Justin, I'd like you to officially meet my best friend, Samantha." He held out his hand, and it took a few seconds for her to respond. She still had stars in her eyes.

Samantha shook his hand. "It's nice to meet you. I'm sorry I was a bumbling idiot earlier."

I patted her shoulder. "Don't worry. He's used to it."

Justin winked at her. "Meghan wasn't that impressed when

she met me. She told me she'd shoot me if I tried to kidnap her."

She grabbed her chest, swooning all over him. "If only I was that lucky."

"Okay, Sam," I said, laughing. "You're acting like an idiot again. Justin's just like any normal guy."

She scoffed under her breath. "Yeah, but with millions of dollars." Money was something I never talked about with Justin. He never flaunted it, which made me respect him even more. Smiling sheepishly, she backed away. "I think I've made enough of a fool out of myself today. I'm just going to go." Her eyes met mine. "I'll tell Emmett you aren't coming to the party this weekend. There's no sense in trying to hook you up when you're already taken."

Justin chuckled and put his arm around me. "It really was nice meeting you, Samantha."

She laughed nervously and smiled at him. "Thanks. And don't worry, I won't tell anyone about you two." Hurrying off, I could tell she was embarrassed as she jumped on her four-wheeler and rushed off.

Justin turned me around and put his arms around my waist. He kissed me and I melted against him. "I'm so sorry about that. I wanted to warn you."

He shrugged. "It's okay. I was more worried about how you were going to take it. I was afraid you wouldn't want to see me anymore once Emmett found out."

That caught me off guard. "Why would you think that?"

He shrugged again, looking uncertain. "He's not going to want you with me, Meghan. If you were my sister, I wouldn't want you anywhere near someone like me. Then again, I tried to keep her away from Dallas, and that didn't work."

I burst out laughing. "Exactly. For however much time we have left, I want to be with you. I don't want to waste a moment of it."

He picked me up in his arms, and I held onto him, yelping. "In that case, let's not waste it."

"What about the fence?" I asked, giggling as he carried me toward the house.

"It'll still be there when we get done."

CHAPTER FOURTEEN

JUSTIN

WINDOWS DOWN, MEGHAN AND I spent the entire day driving through the Grand Teton National Park. There were a ton of people at the different trailheads so we didn't stop, but it was nice to take her out in the truck.

Feet on the dash and eyes closed, Meghan leaned back in the seat, her hair billowing in the wind. Three weeks had passed and not once had we spent a day apart. The only problem was that time was moving way too fast. In just two more weeks, we'd have to say our goodbyes. Never once had she asked to come with me or for me to stay in Wyoming. A huge part of me wanted her to ask, to know that she cared about me as much as I cared about her. Maybe this was my karma for all the bad mistakes I'd made over the years.

There was a good view of Grand Teton up ahead, so I pulled over on the side of the road. A group of bison grazed in the distance, and I took a ton of pictures, making sure to include Meghan in them. Over the past few weeks, I'd snuck pictures of her without her knowledge. I'd even sent a few of them to Callie, who demanded to see what we'd been up to. Basically, she was living vicariously through me since she couldn't travel.

We hopped out of the truck, and I dropped the tailgate so we could sit on it. "Now that we've finished the fence, the barn, and your truck, what are we going to do over the next couple of weeks?" I asked her. She didn't know my birthday was tomorrow. I wanted to take her somewhere, away from Wyoming.

She met my gaze but then focused on her dangling feet. "I don't know. We've already been fishing and hiking on your land a gazillion times. With not being able to really go anywhere, it's hard to find new things to do." She looked over at me and smiled. "Honestly, I don't care what we do. As long as I'm with you, I'm happy."

When she said things like that it gave me hope, but I'd convinced myself not to read too much into it. "What would you say if I told you my birthday is tomorrow?"

Mouth dropping, she shrieked and punched me in the arm. "Oh my God, how could you not tell me that?"

Chuckling, I rubbed my arm. "I'm telling you now."

She clapped, her whole face beaming. That was one of the things I was going to miss about her—she had an energy about her, so full of life. "We have to do something fun. I don't know what, since we can't go out in public, but I'm sure I can come up with something. We could ..."

"Actually," I cut in, "I was hoping you'd go somewhere with me."

Head cocked to the side, her brows furrowed. "Where?"

I held up my hands. "Hear me out before you say no. Since we only have two weeks left, I was thinking we could take a private jet and fly to Turtle Island. I've always wanted to go to Fiji."

Her face lit up, but then it saddened. "Won't the people at the resort see us? What if they take pictures? I don't mind going somewhere with you as long as nobody can find out who I am."

That was when it hit me. I grabbed her hands and pulled her to me. "I got it. I have a friend who owns a private island. His name is Lucas Montgomery. He's a professional golfer. Ever heard of him?"

Her mouth gaped, and she laughed. "My father loves to golf, and Lucas is his favorite. I can't believe you're friends with him. I wish I could tell him all of this." *You could,* I wanted to say, but I didn't want to pressure her.

"Well, it turns out, he bought a private island for his wife before they got married. It was so they could see each other on the down low and enjoy their time together without the paparazzi following them around." Mine and Meghan's story reminded me so much of theirs. Lucas's wife was a doctor that didn't want her reputation tarnished because of his past indiscretions. He was in the same boat I was in at the moment. It turned out well for them, and I had to believe I had a chance.

Meghan's eyes twinkled. "A private island? Must be nice. Where's it at?"

"South Carolina. They named it *Secret Isle*. As soon as we land, I can get him to pick us up and we can take his boat out to the island. No one has to know we're there."

Biting her lip, I could tell she was contemplating it. The pessimistic side of me knew she was going to say no, but the second she grinned and nodded, I knew I'd won. "Hell yeah," I hollered happily. "Let's go pack and get out of here." I jumped off the tailgate and lifted her up in my arms. I kissed her hard and swung her around. "Thank you. This means a lot to me."

My phone rang, and I set her down. She sat back on the tailgate while I pulled it out of my pocket. I figured it'd either be Corey, Callie, or Maddox. Some of the other guys on the team had called every now and again to see how I was, but most of the time I was busy with Meghan to even pick up the phone.

It was Corey.

"Hey, bro," I said, voice elated. I couldn't wait to get Meghan on the beach, all alone on a private island. Lucas had offered it to me before, but I never had anyone special to take there until now.

"Hey," Corey replied. "You sound happy. What's going on?"

"Meghan agreed to fly with me to Lucas' private island for my birthday. I want to leave tomorrow."

The line went silent, and I didn't like it one bit. He knew Meghan didn't want to be seen in public, and I had a feeling he was going to persuade us not to go. Out of this whole ordeal, he'd shown a great interest in Meghan's privacy and making sure I kept her secret, for her sake. I was glad he cared about her, even if he'd never met her. They'd talked on the phone for the first time a couple weeks ago, and they hit it off great.

"Why aren't you saying anything, Corey?"

Meghan clasped her hands in her lap and fiddled with her fingers like she always did when she was nervous. Even though she was a tough woman with a witty tongue, she still had her insecurities, just like me. Corey cleared his throat. "Will you put me on speakerphone so Meghan can hear?"

I did as he said and set the phone on the tailgate so I could hold her hands. That way, she couldn't fidget anymore. I brought them up to my lips and kissed them. "You're good. She can hear you."

"Hi, Meghan," he said.

"Hey, Corey."

He cleared his throat again. "Do you think you two can put off the island vacation for a couple of days?"

"Why?" I snapped, not meaning to sound mad, but he'd better have a pretty damn good reason for us not to go. It was my birthday, after all.

"It's looking like Callie's about to go into labor a little early. She asked me to call you to see if you'd come back home for a couple of days."

Panic settled in my gut. "Is she okay?"

"Yeah, she's fine," Corey assured me.

I didn't want to leave Meghan, especially considering we only had two weeks left together. Meghan could see the turmoil on my face and kissed me. "Go," she whispered. "I'll be here when you come back."

"About that," Corey interrupted. "Callie asked that you come too, Meghan. I know you don't want anyone seeing you, but I have it all planned out. Just wear a hat and sunglasses to be on the safe side."

The wheels in her head turned, but it looked like she wasn't ready to make the decision. "I'll have James here with the jet tomorrow morning. I'll be there no matter what."

"Sounds good, brother. I kind of leaked it to the press that you were in the Turks and Caicos. That should keep them from searching for you when you get here." Hopefully, that would help sway Meghan. "And Meghan, please try to come. I promise, it's not going to be as bad as you think. On the contrary, it's looking like things will be looking up for Justin very soon. I have everything I need to clear his name."

Relief flooded through me. It'd been weeks with nothing but Miranda talking shit about me to the press. Unfortunately, my "disappearance" made me look guilty.

"Fuck me, it's about time. I'll be ready to deal with that when I get home. In the morning, I'll let you know if Meghan's coming with me."

We hung up, and Meghan's face beamed. "You're about to free of the mega-bitch. How does it feel?"

I helped her off the tailgate and pulled her into my arms. "Pretty damn good. It'll be nice to clear my name."

"I bet." She wrapped her arms around my neck, her eyes searching mine. Taking her back to Charlotte with me was risky, and all I wanted to do was beg her to come with me. I wanted her to see the other part of me that I couldn't show her in Wyoming. "Do you honestly think we can get to Charlotte and not be seen by the paparazzi?"

With a heavy sigh, I shook my head. "Maybe when we arrive, but once I deal with Miranda, my whereabouts will be exposed. You'll have to be disguised after that. Apparently Corey has a plan to help. I wish I knew what it was. You'll just have to trust him."

Taking a deep breath, she slowly let it out and smiled. "All right, I'm in. Don't be embarrassed if I pull a Sia and wear a wig over my face."

I burst out laughing. "You could wear a brown paper bag over your face and I wouldn't care. Unfortunately, it would only make the press work harder to find out who you are." Her lips pursed in defeat, but she finished it off with that sexy grin of hers. "Think you can handle it?"

A nervous laugh escaped her lips. "I hope so. I'm meeting your family, Justin. This is huge for me."

I winked. "As long as you don't go drooling around in front of my cousin, Maddox, I'll be fine. The ladies tend to love him."

Clasping her hands on my face, she kissed me long and hard. A car drove by and honked their horn at us. "You have nothing to worry about."

CHAPTER FIFTEEN

MEGHAN

WHAT THE HELL WAS I doing? In just a matter of hours I was going to be on a private jet, headed to North Carolina to meet Justin's family. The thing I was worried most about was the unknown. I had visions in my head of the paparazzi camping out in front of Justin's house to get pictures, but he assured me it wasn't like that all the time. Hell, I wouldn't want that any time.

One of the good things about the trip was that Justin would be able to be free of Miranda, once and for all. Only I had a feeling it wasn't going to be easy. I was almost done packing when Justin knocked on my bedroom door.

"You okay? It's quiet in here."

I folded up the last of my shorts and zipped up my luggage. "Just thinking." He walked in and set my purple suitcase onto the floor so he could lie on the bed. He patted the space beside him and I sat down. "What am I going to do while you're dealing with the Miranda?"

His jaw clenched and anger flashed in his eyes. "I don't plan on wasting much time with her. But while I'm gone, you'll be at my house. You can use the pool, watch a movie in my theater room, or play in the game room. It's all up to you."

Mouth gaping, I stared at him incredulously. "A theater room *and* a game room? How much are you worth, Mr. Money Bags?"

A sly grin spread across his face. "Millions, baby girl."

I could see having that much money being a blessing, but on the flip side, a curse. Kicking off my sandals, I lied down beside him on my elbow. "How does it feel to have that much money? I'll never see that amount in my lifetime."

His smile faded, and he brushed his fingers over my cheek. "It's nice, but it doesn't buy you love or true friends. I'm lucky to have those all on my own." Leaning over, he kissed me softly. "Thank you for coming with me tomorrow. I really wasn't ready to leave you yet."

I held his hand to my cheek. "I know how you feel."

Pressing his lips to mine, he nipped my bottom lip. "Is there anything else you want to know about me before we leave tomorrow?"

There were a million things I wanted to know, the main one being if he was falling in love with me the way I was falling in love with him. It was a question I wasn't ready to ask. If I heard his answer, it could easily change everything between us. I liked what we had, even if I wanted more.

Shaking my head, I grabbed his shirt and pulled him closer. "Kiss me. That's what I want right now."

Everything moved in slow motion, starting when Justin's lips touched mine. My body lit up, hotter than the summer sun. I was on fire, burning from the inside out.

Growing impatient, I moaned breathlessly. "Justin?"

He nipped the tender flesh behind my ear and groaned low in his chest. "Yeah?"

"I want you … now."

His lips stilled against mine, and he pulled back, teasing me with that devilish smile of his. "You sure?"

"Yes," I exclaimed breathlessly. "Unless you'd rather go home with blue balls."

Shifting me in his arms, he wrapped my legs around his waist, and I gasped as he pushed me into the bed. Lifting my hands above my head, he held me prisoner while he bit his way along my collarbone and down to the mounds of my breasts.

"Don't want that," he chuckled, grabbing one of my breasts. He pinched a nipple between his fingers, and I cried out as the sting of pain shot through my body. It felt amazing.

Lifting off me, Justin sat back and slid my shorts and T-shirt off. The fan above us blew air across my bare skin, making me tremble, especially as I watched him stand and undress.

"Sure you know what you're getting into?" I teased. "Last night you seemed worn out after we got done." Truthfully, I was the one worn out. I wasn't used to being with someone every single night. I went from eight years of nothing to full-blown, passionate sex. I craved it.

He winked. "I think I can handle it."

"We'll see about that."

I sat up and slowly glided my fingers down his washboard abs, making sure to slide his boxers down to the ground. His cock was so thick and hard I could barely wrap my hands around him. Holding him tight, I pumped the full length of his cock and licked the tip, rendering a strangled moan from between his lips.

"You're fucking killing me, angel." I let him go, and he hauled me up, until I was standing before him as he sat down on the bed. He closed his lips over a taut nipple and sucked feverishly.

"More," I rasped, arching my back.

"I'll give you more," he growled, kissing his way down my stomach. "But first"—he gently turned me around and pushed me onto the bed—"I want to explore." Goose bumps broke out all over my skin as Justin started at my ankles and ran his hands up the length of my legs. I could feel his breath blow across my skin as he grabbed my ass and leaned in to bite my right cheek.

Using his knee to bump my legs apart, he slowly kneaded my ass, working his way closer to my center. Thumbs reaching between my legs, they rubbed me in a circular motion, as his hands continued to manipulate my flesh.

I let my head fall back as my core tightened. Then he shifted me around quickly, earning a shriek to escape my lips. Not knowing what he was going to do next thrilled me. When his face pushed between my legs and his tongue licked a straight line up and over my clit, I sucked in a huge gasp.

Looking down, we made eye contact, and I almost lost it. Bringing my hands around the back of his head, I raked my fingers through his hair as he tongue-fucked me. Over and over, he licked and sucked my clit until I couldn't take it anymore.

"Give it to me," he commanded. "Let me taste you."

Just hearing his words was my undoing. Grinding against his face, I exploded from the inside out, gripping handfuls of his blond tresses as he tasted every drop of my desire. Grabbing me around the waist, he pulled me onto his lap. I couldn't help but smile. No man had ever made me come that way.

"That felt amazing." My body quivered as it came down from its orgasm-induced high, and Justin was all too happy with my reaction. "I think I'm addicted to your mouth. I want more." His cock throbbed between my legs as I teased him by sliding along its length, only letting the tip inside me.

With short, gentle strokes, I glided up and down, until his grip tightened on my hips and he growled. "You're playing with fire."

Giggling, I lowered down inch by inch until he was completely inside of me.

"You feel so fucking good. I can't believe how wet you are for me." With one hand tugging on my hair, he grabbed a breast with the other. His grip on my hair tightened, and I arched my back, still moving my hips as he ravished my nipples. "Jesus. If you don't stop, I'm going to come." Picking me up by the hips, we stayed connected as he flipped us around and collapsed on top of me.

I wrapped my legs around his waist and held on tight as he thrust his hips deep and hard. Faster and faster he pumped, his lips still suckling on one of my nipples. The harder he sucked and pushed, the closer I came to losing myself; we were both almost to the edge.

"Justin," I cried out.

He growled low in his chest and held on tighter, grunting with his forceful thrusts. "Fuck, you're getting so tight."

Digging my nails into his back, I screamed out my release, and at the same time I could feel him spasm, his cock throbbing as it filled me with his desire. Breathing hard, his body continued to jerk over me with aftershocks, and I watched him come undone.

Completely spent, Justin kissed my neck and rested his forehead to mine. I could've sworn I heard the words *I love you* whispered from his lips, but knowing me, it was just my imagination.

CHAPTER SIXTEEN

JUSTIN

THE MORNING STARTED OFF WITH a bang—literally—and the best birthday breakfast ever. It was a wonderful beginning to what I hoped was a smooth day of traveling to Charlotte. Anything could happen once I was back in the spotlight. There was a meeting scheduled with Miranda in a couple of days, which meant she'd have photographers on hand. She intentionally leaked her whereabouts all the time just so the paparazzi would take pictures of her.

The whole way back home, I loved how fascinated Meghan was about being on a private jet. It was all so new to her, and I liked that she appreciated it. Miranda, on the other hand, was always a cunt to the flight attendants when they offered refreshments. I was a fucking moron for even being willing to tolerate a woman like that. It took a long time to realize that I didn't need a woman with a million dollars in her bank account.

The plane came to a stop, and I grabbed Meghan's hand to help her up. "Where are we?" she asked curiously.

Playfully, I tapped her chin. "We're at a small airport about twenty minutes away from my house. This is the best way to stay off the radar." James came out of the cockpit and opened the plane door. "Come on. My brother should be out there waiting for us."

I grabbed our bags and stopped in front of the pilot. "Thank you for everything, James. I'll be in contact in the next couple of days."

James nodded and held out his hand. "Sounds good, Mr. Davis. Welcome home."

As he said the words, I couldn't help but feel a twinge in my chest as I shook his hand. Charlotte was my home now, but so was Wyoming. How could I ever choose between them? Holding Meghan's hand, we climbed down the stairs, and there, waiting by his silver BMW M6, was Corey.

Meghan squeezed my hand. "Oh my God, you two look so much alike. I'm surprised you're not his twin."

That made me laugh. "We get that all the time."

Corey waved and smiled at Meghan, not me. "Welcome to Charlotte, Meghan. It's nice to finally meet you."

He hugged her, and she giggled. "Same to you."

"Nice to see you too, brother."

Corey let her go and winked. "Sorry, bro. Meghan's a lot prettier than you."

"That she is." I kissed her and set our bags in the trunk of his car. We both hopped in the back, and we were on our way. "How's Callie doing today?" I asked.

Corey glanced at me through the rearview mirror. "Fine. You don't mind if we stop by her house before I drop you off at yours, right?"

"No, that's great. I want to see her." I'd been worried about her and the baby, especially with her still having a couple weeks left of the pregnancy. "Has she talked to Mom and Dad?"

He shook his head. "No, she didn't want to worry them. Plus, she knew Meghan was coming and didn't want her to feel pressured."

Meghan gasped and looked over at me. "She didn't have to do that. I don't want your parents missing the baby being born."

I squeezed her shoulders. "It'll be okay." We arrived at Callie and Dallas' house and there were a couple of cars I recognized in the driveway. Meghan's unsure gaze met mine and I smiled. "It's just Maddox."

"And my fiancée, Hannah," Corey added. "Lacey's here as well, with the baby. They wanted to see you too."

Meghan breathed a sigh of relief and excitement beamed across her face. I liked that she loved kids. Most of the women I'd been with over the years didn't want any because they didn't want to gain the weight or get stretch marks.

Corey parked around the back of the house, and Maddox was in the yard, fixing one of the water fountains in the flower garden. Now that he was retired from the Charlotte Strikers, his hobby was landscape design. "What's up, cocksucker?" I shouted.

Maddox jerked his head around and chuckled. "Happy birthday, man." He jogged over and hugged me. I'd never seen him look so happy.

"Thanks. I'd like you to meet Meghan."

Letting me go, he smiled wide and held out his hand to her. "Ah yes, I've heard a lot about you. Callie's done nothing but talk about the woman who's changed her wild and reckless brother."

Meghan shook his hand and laughed. "I had nothing to do with it. He did that all himself."

Maddox snorted and shifted his gaze to me. "If she only

knew, right?" I glared at him, and he held up his hands. "Okay, I'll be quiet. I'll be inside." I'd talked to him the night before about how I was falling in love with her, and that I didn't know what to do to keep her in my life. He'd told me to tell her everything, and if I didn't, he was going to.

Corey and Maddox walked into the house while Meghan and I followed closely behind. "What was that about?" she whispered.

I rolled my eyes. "Nothing. Maddox can be a pain in the ass sometimes."

I opened the back door, and out of nowhere, shouts erupted from all angles. "*Surprise!*"

There were streamers all across the living room and balloons, all with the number thirty on them. It was just my close family and friends, the people I trusted more than anyone: Corey, Hannah, Dallas, Callie, Maddox and Lacey. Grinning from ear to ear, Callie came out from behind the couch and hugged me. "Happy birthday, Justin." Mouth gaping, I stood there in shock, but a part of me was pissed.

Callie moved over to Meghan and hugged her too. "Thank you so much for coming. You have no idea how much I wanted to meet you."

"So much that you lied to get me here," I grumbled, glancing down at her stomach, which was even bigger than before I left. "Doesn't look like you're going into labor."

Sheepishly, she bit her lip and rubbed her protruding belly. "I know. I shouldn't have lied. It's just, it's your birthday, and you know I like to celebrate them. Plus, it gave me the perfect excuse for you to bring Meghan."

Meghan glared at me, nudging me with her elbow, and my face softened. "It's fine. Next time, don't lie. I was really worried about you and the baby."

Her eyes glistened, and she nodded. "I didn't mean to scare you. I didn't think you'd come otherwise. I really wanted you and Meghan here for your birthday. Besides, you had to come back anyway for the meeting with Miranda's legal team."

Dallas handed me a beer and I huffed. "Don't remind me." I introduced Meghan to the others, and they all seemed really taken with her. Deep down, I was hoping their kindness would work in my favor. Meghan could see how amazing my family and friends were, that my life wasn't all superficial.

"All right, guys," Dallas said, slamming his hands on my shoulders. "Let's get this grill going so we can eat."

Callie linked her arm with Meghan's and waved. "Don't worry, I'll keep her company."

Meghan grinned nervously, but she didn't get a chance to say anything before Callie carted her off. Callie was up to something, only I didn't know what.

CHAPTER SEVENTEEN

MEGHAN

IT WAS ALL SO SURREAL. Dallas and Maddox were famous athletes, and yet, they seemed so normal. Callie had the same blonde hair and green eyes as Justin and Corey. It made me wonder what their brother, Brant, looked like, since he was supposedly the odd one out. Callie's warmth made me feel at home, but I had to wonder what else was up her sleeve for wanting me in town. I could tell Justin was curious about the same thing. Did she not approve of me and wanted me to see how Justin's life was there so I'd know I didn't belong? I hated thinking that way, but I'd seen movies before. My life felt like I was right in the middle of a drama about to unfold.

"While the guys cook the meat, we can hang out and relax," Callie said, leading me into a sun room. "All the other food is done." Hannah followed in behind us and sat down in one of the brown recliners. There was a blonde sitting on the couch, holding a baby that was wrapped snugly in a blanket.

Her eyes lit up when she saw me. "You must be Meghan. Callie told me you were going to be here."

"Lacey?" I asked.

She nodded and grinned wide. "Yep. I'm sure you've already met my knucklehead of a husband."

I sat down in the other brown recliner and laughed. "I did. And I have to say it's pretty crazy being here. My friends back home would lose their minds if they knew." Samantha already did when I called to tell her. She'd told Emmett I was headed to North Carolina, only she didn't tell him what part.

Callie and Lacey looked at each other, almost like there was a silent conversation going on between them. Callie focused back on me, her gaze narrowed curiously. "Most women wouldn't want to keep being with my brother a secret. You have great restraint."

"You know why I am," I replied. "And also, I'm not the type to spread my personal life all over social media."

She nodded, and her smile saddened. "That's what I like about you." Her hand moved between the three of them. "We're all like that. Hannah and I are both nurses, and Lacey is a doctor. We have to maintain a level of professionalism."

Knowing they were normal, just like me, was fascinating. Every time I thought about a professional athlete or a movie star, I always pictured them with other celebrities. That wasn't so. Lacey stood and bounced her little boy gently in her arms. I could see his eyes slowly closing shut.

"Would you like to hold him?" she asked.

I stood and held out my arms, feeling the excitement well up in my chest. Babies were my weakness. "More than anything." She handed me her son; he had dark hair just like his daddy. "What's his name?"

She kissed his forehead and smiled. "We gave him Maddox's name. He's determined to have generations of them so they can all be hockey legends."

The other girls laughed and so did I. I didn't know Maddox very well, but from everything Justin had told me about him, I could totally see him saying that. Carefully, I sat down and held Maddox Jr. in my arms.

"Callie tells me you have a daughter," Lacey said.

I looked over at her and nodded. "Her name's Ellie. She's eight."

"Does she know about you and Justin?" Callie asked.

My chest tightened, and I averted my gaze to the baby. It was amazing how much a parent sacrificed to keep their children safe. "No. I know she'd love him, but I have to be careful." I met their gazes. There was no judgment in the way they looked at me, but I wanted them to understand my reasoning. "I'm aware of the mess Justin's in right now. Even he agreed it was best to keep us under wraps. I don't want the attention or the tabloids running stories about me. I'm a single mother whose husband passed away defending our country. I don't want any false rumors spread about me that my daughter would see. From what I can tell, Miranda's doing a good job of that with Justin."

Lacey and Hannah nodded in understanding, and Callie looked like she was going to cry. Giggling, Lacey passed her a tissue. "Damn pregnancy hormones. Gets you every time." I knew exactly how they felt. I cried all the time when I was pregnant with Ellie, but that was because I'd lost my husband.

Callie held the tissue and sniffled. "I'm ready to feel normal again." She fanned her eyes and when they stopped watering, she sighed. "Meghan, I know you're nervous about people finding out about you. And that's okay. I completely respect your decision. All I'm saying is that my brother has never been happier. I don't want him to lose that...or you. The tabloids and the paparazzi are always going to be around, but we," she said, waving her hand at Lacey and Hannah, "have all gotten through it. You can too. We'll be here to help you."

"I appreciate that, more than you'll ever know. But Justin and I have an understanding. He's going to come back here, and I'll be in Wyoming. I'm going to miss him, but his life is here." It was what I kept telling myself. If I did, it'd help with the pain of him leaving. Baby Maddox cooed, and I smiled down at him. I missed Ellie more than anything, and I couldn't wait to see her again. She was *my* life. I had to think of her wellbeing, not just my own. With a heavy sigh, I looked over at Callie and Lacey. I already knew Hannah and Corey didn't have any kids. "You two are mothers, and with that, you have important decisions to make, not only for yourself but for them as well. With Ellie, her father's gone. She never got the privilege of meeting him. I've stayed single for eight years because nobody I've met could ever be as good as her father." Tears sprung to my eyes. "At least…until I got to really know Justin." I looked away and wiped my face. "But I'm afraid. If Ellie were to get close to someone I was with, and it didn't work out, it wouldn't only be my heart breaking, but hers as well. She's had enough loss. I have to protect her."

The room fell silent, and when I finally got the courage to look at them, they all nodded in understanding. Sheepishly, Callie cleared her throat. "I'm sorry, Meghan. I never thought about it like that. My intention was to get you to see how amazing my brother is. But coming from a mother myself, I can understand your fears. I just know it's going to hurt him to let you go."

My heart already felt his loss. Two weeks wasn't enough time with him. "I know the feeling."

AFTER EATING JUSTIN'S FAMOUS BABY back ribs and Maddox's steak, I was stuffed. Those hockey boys sure knew how to throw down some food. I had to excuse myself so I could call and check on Ellie. She was having a blast, just like I'd hoped. My sister had texted, asking where I was since she could obviously tell I wasn't at home in the video. There was so much I had to tell her when I saw her again.

Over dinner, they all celebrated Justin's birthday by telling embarrassing stories of him as a child. I'd never laughed so hard in my life. Even now, I couldn't get the smile off my face as we headed toward Justin's house. I was curious to see what it looked like.

"Please tell me you're not thinking about the time I got M&M's stuck up my nose or when Callie put makeup all over me while I was sleeping." I tried my best not to laugh, but I couldn't hold it in. Even Corey burst out laughing in the front seat.

"Actually, I was thinking of the time when Maddox replaced your hair gel with glue."

Groaning, he covered his face with his hands. "That was fucking horrible. Had to have my head shaved after that. Couldn't get the shit out."

"And he loved his hair," Corey added. "He was devastated."

Justin shrugged. "I was twelve years old. I had to impress the girls." He winked at me, and I laughed again. "But I got Maddox back. A face riddled in black sharpie before picture day was hell to get off."

I slapped a hand over my mouth. That was devious. "Wow.

That's worse than the glue gel. I'd love to see that yearbook photo of him."

Justin cocked his head, deep in thought. "I can probably get it. My aunt has all of his yearbooks."

Excitement bubbled in my chest, only I hated I wouldn't get to see it. "You should totally get the picture, and next year for his birthday, get him a cake with it printed on top. That'd be hilarious."

Both Corey and Justin doubled over laughing, and Corey said, "I'm afraid my brother's rubbing off on you." We pulled into a wealthy neighborhood with mansions everywhere. Corey glanced back at me and nodded at my hat and sunglasses. "Might want to put those on before you get out of the car. I haven't seen any paparazzi around here in a while, but it's better to be safe than sorry." I did as he said and slipped on my disguise. There was no way anyone would be able to pinpoint who I was if they saw me. I was a nobody.

Justin pointed down the road toward the house at the end, blocked off with a gate. Corey punched in the code and the gates opened. He pulled up to the front of the house and I stared at it, completely transfixed.

"Your house is amazing," I gushed.

We all got out and Justin grabbed our bags. "It's all mine now. Corey and Brant used to live here too until Brant moved back to Minnesota and Corey with Hannah."

Corey glanced up at the house and sighed. "The gate and privacy fence didn't get put up until after Justin was on the show. He gained a lot more popularity after that."

"Did people try coming to your house?" I asked.

A serious expression passed across Justin's face. "For a while, but it stopped after the gate got put in. I've never been in any danger or anything like that." That was a relief, but I couldn't imagine being at home and seeing people on my lawn, taking pictures.

Corey shut the trunk and patted Justin on the back. "I'm out of here, brother. You two have fun tonight. Because the day after tomorrow…"

Justin held up a hand. "I know. I'll be ready."

Corey hugged me one last time before getting in his car and driving away. I took my bag away from Justin and nodded at the door. "I'm ready for a tour."

Justin's smile returned, and I followed him up to the door. When he opened it, I froze at the sight before me. There was a double staircase that came down both sides of the foyer. Up ahead was the living room, and the floor was a gray and white marble that glittered in the light.

"This is so different from your ranch," I said, studying every square inch. There were pictures on the mantel of his family, and up above were two hockey sticks crossed together.

He pointed up at them. "Those were the hockey sticks I used in the last two Stanley Cup playoffs that we won."

I set my bag down, and he did the same. "Do you miss being on the ice? It's been weeks since you put on a pair of skates."

Looking up at the hockey sticks, I could see the longing on his face. "You have no idea how much I miss it."

"Why don't you go to the rink while you're in town?" I said. "I don't mind staying here while you do."

His eyes widened, and he grabbed my hands excitedly. "We can do better than that. I'll call my coach, who owns the skating complex, and get him to open the rink for us tomorrow night, just you and me."

The thought terrified me, but I'd love to see him move on the ice in person. All I'd ever seen him do was on TV. "I will probably break an arm or leg. I haven't skated in years."

Wrapping his arms around me, he kissed me. "I won't let you fall."

"Then it's a date."

"Good. Now let's take you on that tour." Taking my hand, he led me through his kitchen, and all around his downstairs bedrooms. I was curious to see what his bedroom looked like. At the ranch, it was decorated in navy blues and dark greens, but I had a feeling his fancy home was going to be a little more seductive and modern. Instead of taking me upstairs, he opened a door that led down to the basement levels.

"Your bedroom is down there?" I asked.

He shook his head. "Nope. If I take you to my bedroom now, I'll do ungodly things to you. Not that I don't want to right now, but I figured you'd want to see the rest of my house before I take you up there." I followed behind him, and he winked back at me. "This is the fun part of the house."

We turned the corner and there were three doors. He opened the first one, and inside was a large movie theater screen and three rows of recliners. There were even lights lined up at the bottom of the rows like you'd see in a real movie theater. It smelled like popcorn.

"This is amazing. What all movies do you have?"

He opened up his arms. "Anything you want. It's all digital. Maybe tonight we can order some take-out and watch a movie?"

I nodded excitedly and clapped my hands. "I'm totally down for that."

The door across the hall opened up to a gym, and the one at the far end revealed a massive game room. It was like something you'd see in an old arcade. There weren't many of those around anymore, not like there was when I was a kid. Not only were there arcade games, but there were pool and air hockey tables, and then my favorite…a foosball table.

"Oh my God, please tell me you play," I said, rushing over to it.

Justin stood on the other side, grinning devilishly. "I'm the best. Think you can handle me?"

If he only knew. I grew up playing foosball, but I wasn't about to tell him that. "I can hold my own. First one to ten wins?"

He pulled out the small white ball and tossed it in the air. "Sounds good. Want to make it interesting, though?"

"What do you have in mind?"

Tossing the ball up in the air again, he did it over and over with a sly grin on his face. "Instead of going all the way up to ten, why don't we play strip foosball? The first person to take off all their clothes loses."

It was going to be an interesting game. Unfortunately, there wasn't that many articles of clothing on my body since it was summer. I held out my hand and he shook it. "Deal."

He slid the ball down the slot and the game was on. "Spinning the rods is illegal," he said, getting into position.

I rolled my eyes, trying my best to concentrate. "I know, I know."

There was power behind his hits, but I was quick. The ball sailed past his players into the goal. He stared at the table in disbelief, and then over at me. "Damn, angel. That was quick."

I waved a hand at his body. "Take it off."

Slowly and seductively, he took off his shirt and tossed it at me. He'd gotten tanned over the weeks from working on my fence. "How's that?"

"Perfect. You're about to take off more."

Snorting, he put the ball back into play, and we fought over it. I was determined to win. I sunk the ball again, and he took off his shorts. Only one more article of clothing left for him. Justin dropped the ball, and I never took my eyes off of it. We fought back and forth and it almost went into my goal, but I stopped it. That split-second of him celebrating gave me the time I needed. I had a clear opening to the goal.

"*I won,*" I screamed, holding my arms up in the air.

Justin shook his head and huffed. "You hustled me, didn't you? I never lose at foosball."

Batting my eyelashes playfully, I shrugged. "Might want to get used to it."

"Oh yeah?" He lowered his boxers, and my insides clenched with anticipation. Circling the table, he grabbed me around the waist, and I wrapped my legs around him. "Now that I'm naked, what do you want?"

I bit my lip and kissed him. "You."

His cock pressed against me, all hard and rigid as he carried me over to the pool table and set me down. "Looks like we're not going to make it to my bedroom then."

I ran my hands over the green felt and spread my legs. "I'm perfectly fine with that."

CHAPTER EIGHTEEN

MEGHAN

The day went by so fast that everything was a blur. Justin and I went swimming, we watched a movie in his theater, and we talked. The talking was what I loved most about our day. It felt as if each moment that passed, we grew closer and closer.

"Angel, you about ready?" Justin shouted from downstairs.

I was nervous about going out in public, even if the ice rink was closed. It didn't mean that people weren't going to be in the vicinity. I felt stupid for covering myself up as much as I was, but it needed to be done. It was hot outside, but Justin gave me one of his hoodies to put on so I could use it over my head to at least partially obscure my face. I was going to need it inside the skating complex anyway, along with my jeans, to shield my skin from falling all over the ice.

Taking a deep breath, I looked at myself once more in the mirror and hurried downstairs. Justin walked out of the kitchen, eating one of the chocolate chip cookies we'd made earlier. "Doesn't that make the tenth cookie for you tonight?" I asked, laughing. "If I ate like that, I'd be ten thousand pounds."

He winked. "Not with the way I've been working you out." Swirling his keys around his finger, he nodded toward the door. "I figured we'd take my old Bronco. That way, we don't draw too much attention in my sports car."

His blue, convertible Bronco was my favorite out of his collection. We walked out to his garage and hopped inside, the engine roaring to life. I felt stupid for having the hoodie over my head, but I was in the danger zone now. In Wyoming, I wasn't worried as much.

We drove through the town of Belmont, and it looked so nice and quaint. There were people walking up and down the street, going in and out of the shops. "I like this place. It's so different from home."

Justin nodded. "Downtown Belmont is nice. The restaurants are phenomenal."

"What all do you normally do around here?" I asked. "I'm pretty sure fixing fences and painting barns isn't what you do in your free time."

Chuckling, he kept his gaze on the road and reached over to hold my hand. "The guys and I like to hang out at the local pub back there." He pointed at the restaurant we just drove past. It was called Sammy's. "When I'm not there, I'm usually at the rink or at a party. There's always some kind of social function going on." He didn't seem to be enthusiastic about it.

"Doesn't sound like you enjoy it all that much," I said.

He shrugged. "The parties get old after a while. It's not the same. I mainly only went to them to get away from Miranda."

"Are you nervous about the meeting tomorrow?" I was nervous about it, and I wasn't even going to be there. As much as I wanted everything fixed, I didn't want him anywhere near her. She was manipulative. I saw how she wrangled him in her grasp when they were on the show.

The grip he had on the steering wheel tightened. "Corey assures me we have everything we need."

"Good."

He pulled us into the rink parking lot and parked beside a black Escalade. There was a man sitting inside, and I recognized him. He was the Charlotte Strikers' coach, Kellan Carter. Justin got out and came to my side of the car to open the door. "You're safe. I don't see anyone."

I slipped out and Kellan held out his hand. "Hey, Meghan. I'm Kellan."

"Yes, I know," I said, feeling starstruck. "It's so nice to meet you." It was surreal meeting Justin's teammates, especially his coach, who was even more famous than any of the other players.

I shook his hand, and he smiled. "Same to you. Ready to skate?"

Justin wrapped his arm around my shoulders as we walked inside. "Not really. The last time I attempted it, I had bruises for weeks."

"I already told you I'm not going to let you fall."

Kellan unlocked the door and handed Justin the keys. "Lock up when you're done. I'll stop by your house in the morning to get the keys." He held open the door. "Have fun, you two."

Once he was gone, Justin locked the doors. The place was huge. Taking my hand, Justin pulled me to the skate rental booth quickly. I laughed and basically had to run to keep up with him. "I take it you're excited."

"You have no fucking idea. I've been away from the ice way too long."

He jumped over the counter and looked down at my feet, only to do a double take. "You have some big feet."

I smacked his arm. "Thanks. I take after my mom. She's a size eleven as well."

Grabbing our skates, he set them on the counter and hopped back over. I took mine and sat down on one of the benches by the rink. My nerves were shot. I didn't want to look like an idiot fumbling around on the ice, but there was no escaping it. Justin had his skates on within seconds and then came over to lace mine up since I was taking so long.

When he was done, he helped me up. "Here we go." Palms sweaty, I held him tight as he stepped onto the ice and pulled me with him. He glided across the ice so fluidly, while I had no doubt I looked like a statue. He skated in front of me, holding both of my hands.

Justin tried his best not to laugh and failed. "You have no idea how ridiculous you look. The ice isn't going to kill you. Move your feet." Taking a deep breath, I concentrated on his movements and tried to mimic him. He let one of my hands go and dropped back beside me. We did one lap around the rink, then another, and another. "You're doing good, angel."

My grip loosened on his hand as we did a few more rounds. "Let me go," I told him.

"You sure?"

I looked over at him. "Yes. If I fall, you can pick me up."

"Always." His smile made the butterflies come back. I'd missed that feeling. With him, I felt them every day.

Ever so slowly, he let me go. I wobbled on my feet for a second, but I did it. I was skating on my own. At least, until my ankles twisted and I felt myself falling. Justin grabbed me around the waist, and we spun around the ice until we bumped into the rink wall. Heart racing, I grabbed my chest. "Holy shit, that could've ended bad."

Justin chuckled and kissed me. "Told you I'd catch you."

I patted his chest. "You know what. Why don't you skate around for a while and I'll watch you? I want to see your skills." I didn't want him having to babysit me around the ice all night. He needed to let loose.

His face lit up and he helped me off the ice to one of the benches. "Have a seat and I'll be right back."

He disappeared down the back hallway and came back with a hockey stick and puck. The excitement on his face reminded me of a kid at Christmas. In Wyoming, I never got to *see* his love for the ice. I could only hear about it. He zoomed around the rink, handling the puck precisely. I took a few pictures of him, and even snuck a couple of videos. I wanted to capture every single memory with him.

My phone rang and I fumbled to get it out of my pocket. I'd already talked to Ellie so I knew it wasn't her since it was way past her bedtime. It turned out to be Grant. "Hey," I answered.

In a sing-song voice, he asked. "So…what are *you* doing right now?"

I was immediately on high alert. "Nothing, really. Why?"

"Well, I stopped by your house and you weren't there. Then, I went to the store to grab some ice cream. The line was long so I stood there and read through some of the tabloids. When that got old, I pulled out my phone."

I froze and held my breath. Was he implying something? My stomach clenched, and my eyes immediately went to Justin. His brows furrowed, and he skated over to me. "Okay. Why are you telling me that?" Justin mouthed the words *what's wrong*, but I held up my hand.

"Because I saw something on my phone that caught my attention. Or better yet, *someone*. I saw his face and I was like…he looks familiar. I couldn't place it until I saw the girl next to him."

Closing my eyes, I hung my head. "And?"

"*And everything, Meghan.* It's you in the freaking picture. You're wearing Trey's favorite baseball cap. What the hell are you doing with Justin Davis? And nice touch, by the way, on the hiking trail. He had me fooled."

Desperation flooded through my veins. "Other than the hat, can you tell it's me?" Justin rushed over and bent down on his knees in front of me. Grant could obviously hear the panic in my voice.

"Calm down, Meg. No, you can't see your face. I only recognized Justin because there's a clear shot of his face. Then with you next to him, I put two and two together."

Justin squeezed my hands and I met his gaze. "There's a picture of us in the tabloids."

Taken aback, he stood. "What? Where?"

"Grant, I'm putting you on speakerphone," I said.

Grant cleared his throat. "It was right in front of your house, Justin. You were both standing next to a BMW. The online article was talking about your many flings and how much trouble you were in with the TV producers."

Justin's fiery eyes met mine, but then he looked away and growled. "That fucking bitch. She knew I was going to be in town so she had someone waiting on me."

"I take it you're wanting to keep your relationship a secret?" Grant asked.

Sighing, I took him off speakerphone. "Yes. He's going through a lot with his ex-fiancée, and I didn't want to be dragged into it. Not to mention, I don't want Ellie having to deal with it either."

Grant's voice softened. "I get it, Meghan. When are you coming back home?" I knew he'd understand.

"Soon. I'll tell you everything. Just keep all of this to yourself."

"I will." We said our goodbyes, and I set my phone down on the bench. It was a lot to process.

"Meghan?" I looked up at Justin, his expression torn. "I'm so sorry. What can I do?"

It wasn't his fault. We just had to be even more careful. "It's okay. Grant recognized you and then put two and two together. He wouldn't have guessed it, otherwise."

Justin's phone rang, and he jerked it out of his pocket. "Yeah," he answered, running a hand angrily through his hair. "We already know. Meghan's friend from Wyoming recognized us." He looked over at me. "No, she's fine. We'll just be on guard and make sure no one can see her face." Fists clenched, he leaned against the rink wall. There was so much fire and anger in his eyes. "I agree. This shit ends tomorrow." He ended the call and helped me up, pulling me tight into his arms. "Whatever you do, don't let this scare you away from me. We have two weeks left, and I don't want that to end because of this. I'm going to get it all handled tomorrow ... I promise."

Lying my head against his chest, I could hear his heart beat. I was scared of people finding out who I was, but my need to be with him was greater. All I had to do was keep hidden; I could do that. I wasn't about to give up the next two weeks.

"I'm not going anywhere," I whispered. "And tomorrow, make sure you nail Miranda's ass to the wall. She can't get away with what she's done to you."

An evil chuckle vibrated in his chest. "Don't worry, angel. She has no idea what she's in for."

CHAPTER NINETEEN

JUSTIN

"YOU READY FOR THIS?" COREY asked. The meeting was supposed to be private, but waiting outside the courthouse were camera crews and reporters. *Fucking Miranda.* Always wanting her face in the spotlight. "David texted and said he's already inside and so is Tony."

David Correll was my attorney, and Tony Romano was the private investigator and former FBI agent who'd found out all the dirty details I needed to bust both Miranda and her father. Miranda and her father pulled up in their limo and started up the stairs, right through the camera crews, smiling as if they already won.

My phone beeped with a text, and I smiled.

Meghan: You got this. Good luck!

"Hell yeah, I'm ready. Let's go." We got out and walked

right past the cameras. The reporters spat out questions left and right, but I wasn't about to give away that I was going to win. Miranda was about to get the surprise of her life.

Once in the courthouse, the officer at the door directed us on where to go. We turned down the long hallway, and standing outside was David and Tony. David held out his hand, and I shook it. He was thirty-three years old, dressed in an expensive Armani suit with his brown hair slicked back. He'd handled a lot of high-profiled cases and won all of them.

"It's good to see you again, Justin." He nodded toward the room. "I'm going to go in and get all my notes together. Do me a favor and let Tony and I do most of the talking. The last thing we want is you losing your cool. There's no need to, since we have the upper hand." Miranda was inside, grinning smugly, with her father beside her. He was a prick to everyone around him. There were so many times over the past year that I wanted to punch the shit out of him.

"Be right there," I said.

He disappeared inside, and Tony held out his hand. He was middle-aged, with salt-and-pepper hair, and muscles twice as big as mine. "I am a big fan, Mr. Davis. Hockey's my favorite sport."

I shook his hand. "Thanks, Tony. And I'm a big fan of yours. Without you, I wouldn't have a case."

Tony patted my shoulder and winked. "You should've seen the people pissing their pants after I got done with them. You would've loved it."

"Yes, I would." Chuckling, we all three entered the room and took the seats across from Miranda and her father. Her lawyer sat on one end of the mahogany desk and David on the other.

Miranda's father glared at me with his beady eyes while she still continued to smile. Her perfume filled the air, and she had on a ton of makeup, like usual. The more I stared at her, the more I realized I was a fucking idiot to have chosen her. I should've exposed the show for what it was—tell everyone that I had no choice but to choose Miranda because her daddy made it so. All I wanted was to get into show business, but this was a price I never should have been willing to accept.

Miranda's lawyer cleared his throat and opened the folder he had in front of him. "We're still waiting on Tom Branfield to show, but I'm going to go ahead and get started." Tom was the TV producer for *Rich and Single*. "For those of you who don't know, my name's Harold Forsyth. I'm here on behalf of Miranda and Stan Davenport, and Tom Branfield." He fiddled through his notes and pulled out a piece of paper. "It appears that Mr. Justin Davis has violated his contracts and caused my client emotional distress. We're here to collect damages in the amount of five million dollars to Ms. Miranda Davenport, and five million to the producers of *Rich and Single* for breaking contract." He passed a stack of papers over to David, who in return showed them to me. It was one of the contracts I signed before the show even started, not the one where it was amended to Miranda being chosen the winner.

"Nice," I snapped, doing my best to keep from jumping over the table and punching the smile off of Stan's face. "Where's the contract I signed after you paid off the producers to make your daughter the winner?"

Stan sat up straighter and scoffed. "You have no idea what you're talking about."

His lawyer paused and glanced back and forth at us. "Other contract? Am I missing something?"

Stan waved a hand dismissively at me. "He's just angry he got caught cheating on my daughter. We have all the proof we need."

"Yes, we do," David announced, bringing out his own stack of papers. He tossed them over to Stan and handed a set to Harold. "You didn't honestly think Tom Branfield burned the copies of this like you paid him to, did you? That contract is an amendment to the original one, stating that Miranda was to be the winner. The show was rigged."

It was my turn to gloat. Miranda and Stan looked at each other, panic clearly on her face. Stan crinkled up the contracts and threw them across the table at David. "Doesn't matter. It's still in the contract that one year after the show, both parties are to remain faithful to the other, no matter if they're together or not."

Harold sighed and focused on me. "I was not aware of this amendment, but he's correct—even the amendment contains that language. From my records, you have five indiscretions. It's clearly a violation." He held up all the different tabloids, showing me with various women. It had to have been pictures taken before I even appeared on the show. Even my hairstyle was different in them.

David placed a hand on Tony's shoulder. "Sorry, but there were no violations. I'm going to let Mr. Tony Romano take over."

Tony stood and winked at me before turning his evil glare to Miranda and Stan. "Not that you care, but I'm Tony Romano, former FBI agent and private investigator." Miranda's face paled, but she still managed to keep that chin up in the air like she was better than everyone else. Tony slid his file across the table. Neither Miranda or Stan bothered to look inside. "What I have there are copies of the pictures used in the tabloids over the last few weeks. You say that Mr. Davis violated the contracts, but those photos were taken long before he ever met Ms. Davenport. I've been in contact with each photographer, and they were able to give me specific dates and times on when they were taken."

He nodded for them to look inside, but they refused. Eyes wide, Harold reached for the folder and frantically searched through it all. Tony turned to him. "I'll continue while you look. You'll also find bank statements in there as well. There's a rather large deposit to Tom Branfield from Mr. Davenport."

Stan slammed his hands on the table. "You can't prove that it has anything to do with this matter."

Clenching my teeth, it took all I had to keep quiet. It wasn't in my nature not to defend myself. Unfortunately, we weren't on the ice. If we were, Stan would be missing a few teeth and have a hockey stick up his ass.

Tony slung his head back and chuckled. I really liked the guy. "What is it with you rich people? You're so delusional, always thinking that nothing can touch you." He placed his hands on the table and leaned over toward Stan. "Do you want to know why Tom Branfield isn't here? It's because I got his bank information directly from him. He's willing to testify against you if this ridiculous case goes to court. The same thing goes for the young ladies who took money from your daughter. I have their bank information as well, with large sums given to them directly from a Miranda Davenport." Tony turned to Miranda and smiled. "Might want to reconsider pursuing this whole thing. You got dumped. Get over it and move on."

Mouth gaping, she jumped out of her seat. "How dare you talk to me like that? This is bullshit. I demand compensation. Justin made me look like an idiot on live TV."

Tony scoffed and leaned over to me. "Bet that wasn't hard," he mumbled.

I turned my head to keep from showing my smile. It pissed Miranda off even more. She grabbed up a handful of papers and threw them on the floor. "How could you be so cruel? After all we shared together."

"Sit down, Miranda," Stan snapped. His shoulders sagged, and he looked defeated as he rubbed his forehead.

"Mr. Davenport?" Harold called out. "We don't have a case here. Not to mention, it's hard to represent clients who withhold pertinent information." He turned to David and nodded. "How would you like to proceed?"

Clearing his throat, David stood behind me. "First off, there were clearly no violations to the contracts. It will be the responsibility of Miranda Davenport to make a formal statement, clearing Justin Davis from all accusations. If you fail to do so, we'll sue you for damages of five million dollars."

Tears fell down her cheeks, and she shook her head. It was the first real emotion I'd ever seen from her. "That'll ruin me...my career."

"Maybe you should have thought about that sooner," I snapped angrily.

David squeezed my shoulders, and I bit my tongue. "Also, if any scandalous or questionable stories of Justin Davis appear in the tabloids, Miranda Davenport will be thoroughly investigated. If proven guilty, you'll be sued for two million dollars per story." Silence filled the room, and neither Miranda nor Stan would look at me. Their guilt was written all over their faces.

Blowing out a triumphant sigh, I stood. "Now that all of that's over, I hope you all have a great day." I turned my attention to Harold. "I expect your client to make a formal statement today, clearing my name." He nodded, and that was it. I took off out the door and breathed a sigh of relief. It was done. My nightmare with Miranda was over.

"Incoming," Corey warned behind me.

I turned around and Miranda stormed over to me. "Who is she?"

"Who's who?" I shouted, throwing my arms in the air.

"The girl at your house."

"That's none of your fucking business. What'd you do, hire someone to stake out my house until I got back into town? Have you no shame at all, woman?"

The intake of her breath echoed all around us. Everyone

walking around the courthouse froze and watched us. She poked a finger against my chest. "You chose me, Justin. How did you expect me to react after you dumped me on live TV? No matter what the contracts said, you chose *me.*"

"I did," I answered truthfully. "And it was the biggest mistake of my life." I pointed at the reporters, waiting outside of the courthouse. "I look forward to hearing you speak the truth for once."

Turning on my heel, I walked out the front door and smiled.

CHAPTER TWENTY

MEGHAN

All morning, I'd lounged at the pool, swimming and floating around in the inflatable lounger. I checked my phone constantly for updates from Justin, but none came.

"It's about time you got a chance to catch up with me," my sister scolded. "I've been dying to ask you about the picture I saw of you and Justin. What's going on?"

Groaning, I lied back on the lounge chair, my skin hot from the sun. "You noticed it too?"

"Only because you were with Justin. Nobody can see your face. What I want to know is what's going on with Miranda. Have you heard anything?"

I shook my head. "Nothing. I'm still waiting. Justin assured me he had all the proof he needed."

"What happens after his name is cleared, and Miranda's no longer a threat? Think you'll go public with your relationship?"

"Yeah, right," I laughed incredulously. "In two weeks, he'll be back to his hockey life, and I'll be in Wyoming. What kind of relationship works when you can see each other three months a year?"

"Have you asked him what he thinks about it?"

I'd wanted to, but always chickened out. There was no other option. "No," I answered. "Either way, there's nothing that can be done. I'm going to enjoy my time with him while I have it, and that's it."

"Something tells me you won't be okay with that when the time comes."

I had to be. "Doesn't matter. It is what it is."

"Keep telling yourself that." I could hear my mother's voice in the background, calling for her. "Meghan, I have to go. We're taking the girls back out to the beach."

"Tell Ellie I'll call her tonight." Words couldn't even begin to describe how much I missed her.

"I will." We hung up, and I jumped back into the pool and onto the inflatable lounger. Closing my eyes, I breathed in deep and let it out slow. My sister was right; I wouldn't be okay when Justin and I had to part ways. It was going to break my heart. I kept waiting for him to tell me it would all be okay and that we'd figure it out, but he hasn't. We haven't even talked about any kind of future beyond two weeks from now. All I knew was that I wasn't going to be the first one to bring it up. I was terrified at the thought of it.

"Angel!"

Gasping, I jerked up, and the lounger rocked beneath me. "Out here!"

Justin appeared in the back doorway, his button-down shirt open and tie in disarray. He ran down to the pool, his face full of excitement. After ripping off all his clothes, he jumped in the water, butt naked. I squealed when he came up underneath me and tipped me over. His hands grabbed me around the waist, and he pushed me to the side of the pool.

"Oh my God!" I shrieked. "What are you doing?"

I wrapped my legs around his waist and held onto him. His lips pressed against mine, and he pushed his body against me. "It's done. We totally fucked Miranda and her dad in the ass."

"So it's over?" I asked.

He beamed. "Yep. My name is clear, and she gave a statement to the press saying that I did nothing wrong."

"That's awesome. Do you think she'll leave you alone now?"

There was doubt on his face, but he played it off. That worried me. From what I could tell on TV, Miranda had a psychotic, jealous streak. "She has to," he said. "If she doesn't, I'll get a restraining order on her. That'll screw her career up even more." He kissed me again. "Don't worry about her. Nobody knows who you are, and we'll keep it that way."

I nodded. "Okay."

"Enough about her. Right now, we need to celebrate." He trailed his lips across my cheek and down my neck. Chills broke out on my skin, and I shivered.

"What do you have in mind?"

He backed me up against the pool wall and held onto the edge before lowering his lips to mine. They were so soft and firm. Everything inside of me tightened. Willingly, I opened for him, and he pushed his tongue inside with demand, like he *needed* me ... I loved it. He untied my bikini bottoms and tossed them onto the lounge chair.

"Does that answer your question?" he teased. Next, he untied my top and lifted me up so he could suck a taut nipple between his lips.

"Yes," I breathed. "Yes, yes, and yes." I wanted him so bad I couldn't even think straight. I could feel the tip of him at my opening, just slightly pushing in. Squeezing him with my legs, I tried to sit down on him, but he wouldn't let me.

Chuckling, he bit my nipple, and I yelped. "I thought you wanted to celebrate. Teasing me doesn't count."

He flicked his tongue across my nipple and smiled. "No, but it's fun to watch you squirm." Grabbing his face, I kissed him hard and then lowered a hand between his legs. I slid my hand up and down his cock, earning a strangled moan.

"Who's squirming now?"

Groaning, he pushed inside of me. "You're killing me, angel. You have no idea how much I love being able to feel you like this." Slowly and gently, our hips rocked together in perfect rhythm until he stopped and smiled at me.

"Why'd you stop?"

He bit his lip. "I think it's time to heat things up a bit."

"Oh yeah? How so?"

Without answering, he gripped my waist with his strong hands and lifted me off his length, turning me around. I gasped with how quick he moved me, my heart thumping wildly in my chest when he lowered his lips to my ear, biting down.

"You're going to want to hold onto the edge, angel. This might get a little rough."

Instantly, my insides tightened in anticipation, and my nipples grew more sensitive. I held onto the edge of the pool as he snaked his arms around me, pushing his rigid cock between my legs and pinching my nipples between his fingers. I squeezed my legs around him, and he used my breasts to pull me up and down his length. I could feel my orgasm beginning to build, and the moment my body clenched down, Justin changed angles and slammed his cock inside of me.

I bit my lip to keep from crying out as he rode me hard, rubbing his thumb achingly fast across my clit. The water sloshed around us, and I was about to lose my hold on the edge of the pool, but Justin's grip held me firmly in place. His thrusts went deeper and deeper, until it was too much to bear.

"Fuck, angel," Justin grunted. "I'm gonna come."

Hearing him say that was my undoing; it was too late to hold back. The harder he pushed, the harder I came, trembling all around him. My orgasm went on and on, getting stronger the second Justin dug his fingers into my hips and yelled out, cock pulsing as he came inside of me.

Breathing hard and jerking with aftershocks, Justin kissed the back of my neck and rested his head against mine. "You know what would make this night even better?"

"What?"

"Food."

Laughing, I pushed my ass into him. "Perfect. You made me hungry. Then after we eat, we can go for round two."

JUSTIN LEFT FOR THE STORE to grab us stuff to make dinner with while I stayed back to take a shower. When I got out, I heard him downstairs, moving around. "That was fast," I shouted. I ran the towel through my hair and threw on a pair of shorts and the T-shirt he had on this morning before he left for court. It smelled just like him. My stomach growled so I hurried down the stairs. "Hope you got something good. I'm starving."

I turned the corner to the kitchen, expecting to see Justin, but was in for the shock of my life. Miranda stood there, dressed in a skintight red dress and heels, holding my license. "Hello, Meghan."

"What the hell are you doing here?" I was right. She was a psycho.

She held up her hands. "No need to get angry. I just stopped by to grab some of the things I left here."

Anger welled up in my chest. I didn't have my phone close by to call the police. "More like broke in. There's something seriously wrong with you. Get out before I call the police."

Rolling her eyes, she tossed me a key. "Technically, I didn't break in. I won't be needing that anymore." Her focus landed back on my license. "Meghan Taylor. Thirty-one years old from Wyoming. You're a long way from home, aren't you?"

"That's none of your damn business."

She snorted. "That's exactly what Justin said when I asked about you. I was wondering who you were." She tapped my license. "Now I know." Her gaze roamed up and down my body. "Not really anything to look at, are you?"

"Obviously, it was enough to make you break in. Let me guess, you're going to go screaming to the tabloids about how hideous Justin's new girlfriend is." That would be my worst nightmare. I let my anger take over, and it helped with the fear. Miranda could ultimately ruin me.

Miranda scoffed and tossed my license on the kitchen counter. "Please. I'm not going to waste my time on you or Justin."

"Then why do you care? Move on." Not that anyone would have her, now that she proved to be a crazy bitch.

"Oh, I plan to, honey. I was just curious to see who took my place. From what I can tell, you're a nobody. Probably a stripper he met at the bar last night."

"Get out," I growled, taking a step toward her. She didn't like that. Women like her were all bark and no bite. Unfortunately, I couldn't physically kick her out because knowing her, she'd sue me, even if she did practically break in. I couldn't afford it either way.

"Men like Justin don't stay with one woman for long. Has he told you he loves you?" Chest tight, I froze. I'd been waiting on those words, but he had yet to tell me. Her grin widened, and she laughed. "Didn't think so. He's happy at the beginning, but then he gets bored. Might as well get out now before he breaks your heart."

My blood boiled, and I slammed my hand down on the kitchen counter. She shrieked and scrambled back toward the door. "So help me God, get the hell out of here right now, or I'll rip off your anorexic-looking arms and shove them up your ass!" She hurried out the door, and I slammed it so hard behind her that the doorframe shook.

Hands shaking, I leaned against the door, taking short, slow breaths to calm myself down. Nothing worked. I wasn't about to listen to anything that sea donkey had to say, but I couldn't ignore the pang in my chest. Justin hadn't said he loved me and vice versa. I wanted to, but it never felt like the right time. Deep down, I was afraid I'd come off too needy. With Trey, nothing was hard. We were both from Wyoming, and we loved the same things. Our relationship came so easy to us. With Justin, I had everything on the line. Everything about our relationship was difficult.

Looking around Justin's house, at all the fancy furniture and how enormous it was, it finally dawned on me that it wasn't mine. It was all a fantasy, one that could easily be taken away. Hurrying up the stairs and to the bedroom, I packed my bag and sat on the bed. Was I doing the right thing? Hell if I knew, but I had to protect myself and my heart. Justin and I were going to have to say goodbye in two weeks anyway. Maybe now I could get a head start in dealing with my inevitable heartbreak.

I called for a cab and walked down to the kitchen. There

was a notepad on the counter so I grabbed a pen and scribbled a quick note.

Dear Justin,
I'm sorry, but I have to do this.
Meghan

CHAPTER TWENTY-ONE

JUSTIN

I WAS SO HAPPY, I FELT like I was walking on air. Everything was perfect. The lady at the register smiled at me as I came into her line. Her name was Kathryn, and I tried to get in her line every time I went into the store. She was in her late-fifties, with red hair that she'd braid down her back. What I loved about her was that she treated me like every other customer.

"Good afternoon, young man," she said, scanning my groceries.

"Good afternoon, Kathryn. Are you having a good day?"

She winked at me. "Now I am. Haven't seen you at all the past few weeks."

I pulled out my wallet and slid out my credit card. "Yeah, I've been out of town. I needed a vacation."

"I bet." After scanning all of the food, she reached into the cart and grabbed the flowers. She smiled wider as she rang them up. "Someone special?"

"You could say that." I was going to lay everything on the line tonight and tell her how I felt, that I loved her. I was nervous just thinking about it, but it was time I took that step. What worried me was that she'd think I was moving too fast. I didn't want to ruin what we had by trying to move things in a different direction.

Kathryn placed the grocery bags of food in the cart, along with the flowers. "Good luck, Justin. Whoever she is, she's a lucky girl."

I shook my head. "I'm a lucky guy."

I carried everything out to my car and started on my way back home. I'd been gone a lot longer than expected, but hopefully, I could smooth things over with the flowers. When I got home, I pulled into my open garage and went through the kitchen door.

"Angel, I'm back! Sorry it took so long!" I put the groceries away and grabbed the flowers. She hadn't answered me, which probably meant she was in the shower. However, when I turned the corner to the living room to head upstairs to surprise her, I stopped dead in my tracks. Sitting on my couch in a short red dress and heels was Miranda, grinning like the evil thundercunt she was. "What the fuck are you doing here?" My eyes instantly shot upstairs to my hallway, where I prayed to God Meghan didn't come out.

Miranda stood and waved her hand dismissively in the direction of my bedroom. "Don't worry, Meghan's not here. She left in a cab about ten minutes ago. I came to get the diamond earrings I left here." She held up the earrings and batted her eyelashes innocently.

It was as if everything came crashing down. Miranda knew who Meghan was, she broke into my house, and had most definitely said some vile things to her. Rage boiled in my veins, and I dropped the flowers, clenching my fists so hard my fingers went numb.

"What did you say to her?" I didn't even recognize the sound of my own voice. I was so fucking angry I couldn't see straight.

Miranda smiled down at the flowers and laughed. "Guess you really like this Meghan. You never got me flowers."

"It's because you're a hateful bitch that only cares about herself. Now tell me what you said to her, dammit!" I demanded through clenched teeth.

She shrugged. "Nothing really, just that you get bored easily. I didn't know she was going to pack up and leave with me saying that." Pursing her lips, she shook her head disapprovingly. "Kind of a sad. Didn't think you liked weak women."

"She's not weak," I growled. "You're jealous that she's everything you're not."

Her laugh made my ears hurt. "Me, jealous? Yeah, right. She has nothing on me. From the second I looked at her, I could tell she was a nobody. People like you and me can't date normal people. It never works."

I shook my head. "Wrong. Nothing will ever work with you because you're a desperate whore who'd fuck anyone and everything just to get ahead." I'd never spoken to a female like that before, and I didn't like doing it, but it had to be done.

Miranda's mouth gaped, and she fumed. "I'm glad she left. You don't deserve to be happy after what you did to me." She stormed off toward the front door and opened it, but I slammed it shut.

"Actually, I do." Sliding my phone out, I called the police. "I don't know what you said to Meghan, but I'm going to make sure you pay for everything you've done."

THE POLICE HAD TAKEN MIRANDA away, and I'd made sure the photographers were here to watch. I didn't feel sorry for her one bit. For good measure, I put a restraining order out on her and made sure it included Meghan as well. I didn't want Miranda getting anywhere near her.

For the past hour, I'd called Meghan over and over, but she didn't answer. I left her a shit-ton of messages and still nothing. There was no trace of her at my house, other than the note she left. That wasn't good enough. I needed to know why she left.

Grabbing the keys to my fastest sports car, I hopped inside and sped out of my driveway. Meghan could be at the airport or on her way to the Outer Banks. I had no fucking clue which way to go. Before I could get on the interstate, I pulled over into the gas station and tried Meghan one more time. I prayed to God she answered. It rang and rang, and I was prepared to leave another message when her voice spoke on the other end.

"Hey." Voice raspy, I could tell she'd been crying. It sounded like she was in a car, not in the airport.

"Meghan, I don't know what Miranda said to you, but please come back to me. We need to work this out."

She sniffled and blew out a heavy breath. "No. I didn't leave because of what of Miranda said. I'm not that stupid to believe anything that came out of her mouth. Although, I did want to punch the shit out of her."

That did nothing to help the ache in my chest. "I don't understand. Why'd you leave?"

"Someone was going to have to, Justin. Miranda breaking into your house like it was normal made me realize that your world is completely messed up. I've never had to deal with psychotic exes and people getting away with breaking and entering just because they have money."

"She didn't get away with anything, Meghan. The police came and took her away. I got a restraining order out on her."

She gasped, and it was the first time I heard a small level of excitement in her tone. "Good. Maybe now she won't feel so invincible."

"Does that mean you'll come back?" I asked, hoping and praying she said yes.

"I miss my daughter, Justin. This fairytale we've lived in the past few weeks is just that, a fairytale. I have responsibilities that are waiting for me. One way or another, this had to end. It's best we end it now before—"

"Before what?" I said, interrupting her. "Before it's too late? Sorry, angel, but that's not how this works."

"I'm not the kind of person you're used to, Justin. Models and socialites understand the kind of life you live. I don't. Normal for me is waking up in flannel pajamas with my little girl right beside me and going to work to teach my fifth-graders."

"And you think that's something I don't want? Why do you think I've been with you all this time?"

She sighed. "I don't know. I was hoping that maybe you ..."

"That I what? *Loved* you?" The line went silent, and my heart stopped. I wanted to say it a thousand times to her, but I didn't know if she was ready to hear it. I refused to wait any longer.

"Doesn't matter," she whispered, "there's nothing we can do about it. Your life is there, and mine is in Wyoming with my daughter. It would never work."

"Yes, it will. We can make it work. I—"

I was about to tell her I loved her, but she cut me off. "No, don't. It's over, Justin. We have to let each other go." She let out a sad, ragged breath. "I'm sorry." And that was it. She hung up, and I sat there, holding the phone to my ear. I didn't get the chance to tell her I loved her, but I'll be damned if I'd let it end like that.

Tossing my phone in the seat, I sped out of the gas station and over to Callie's house. Dallas was outside cutting the grass when I pulled in. He hopped off the riding mower and wiped the sweat off his forehead with his shirt. "Dude, you look like shit. What's wrong?"

"It's Meghan. She left, and I don't know what to do."

He shook his head. "What'd you do?"

I closed my eyes. "It's what I didn't do, I think. Plus, Miranda broke in and said some evil shit to her. Now she's gone, and I want her back."

Patting my shoulder, he nodded toward the house. "Callie's in there watching TV. She'll know exactly what you should do."

I hurried inside and found her asleep on the couch, a bowl of grapes resting on her large stomach. Ever so gently, I sat down on the other end and tickled her foot. She jerked awake, and the grapes went flying in the air.

"Oh, my God," she shrieked. She grabbed her chest with one hand and slapped me on the arm with the other. "You scared the crap out of me." My smile faded, and her brows furrowed. "What's wrong? Where's Meghan?"

With a heavy sigh, I leaned back against the couch. "She left. Miranda broke in and said some things to her, and she bailed. Left me a note saying she was sorry."

"What?" she growled, her face turning bright red. "If I wasn't pregnant, I'd beat the snot out of her."

"Snot? Really?"

She rubbed a hand soothingly over her stomach. "I have to

watch my language around the baby. I don't want her coming out and saying bad words." She waved impatiently for me to continue. "Now tell me everything."

I shrugged. "I'm pretty sure she's driving to the Outer Banks to be with her family. She told me about her responsibilities and how it would never work between us. I tried to tell her it would and that I loved her, but she hung up. Every time I call now it goes straight to voicemail." Gaze narrowed, she studied me, and I held up my arms. "What?"

"How do you know it would work between you two?"

"Because I know. I love her, and I'm willing to do whatever it takes."

She shook her head. "She's going to kill me for saying this, but has she even told you her biggest fear?"

That took me aback. "What do you mean?" I asked.

Reaching over, she grabbed my hands. "While you and the guys were working on the grill, Meghan was with us in the back room. She said something to us that really got me thinking. I don't think you know."

I squeezed her hands and let go. "What'd she say?"

Her gaze landed on her stomach, and she smiled. "Being a mother changes you, Justin. You have a little person that depends on you for everything. Meghan's situation is harder because she's a single mother, whereas I have Dallas. If you want a future with Meghan, you have no choice but to take on a father role for Ellie. That means you have to be in her life."

I nodded. "Exactly. I've heard her and Meghan talking, and she's funny and sweet, just like Meghan. I'd give anything to meet her."

"Have you told Meghan that?"

"No," I said, averting my attention to the floor. "I was afraid it'd scare her off."

"That's where you need to figure things out. If you want to be a part of Meghan's life, you need to show her that you're not scared. She's afraid that if your relationship fails, it won't just break her heart but Ellie's as well. That's why she was prepared for you guys to go your separate ways." She brushed a hand down my arm, and I met her gaze. "She just wants to protect her daughter, even if she has to sacrifice the love of her life. Believe me, I'd be the same way."

"Then tell me … what would you want the love of your life to do if this was your situation."

Her lips pulled back in a sad smile. "In your heart, you already know. You're a good man, Justin. And you have a kind heart, even if you have made some horrible decisions in your life. This is a choice you have to make on your own. As much as you love Meghan, I don't think you'll go wrong."

It was as if everything fell into place. I knew where I needed to be, and I wasn't going to let anything stop me.

CHAPTER TWENTY-TWO

MEGHAN

BY THE TIME I REACHED Nags Head, my eyes were like sandpaper. I'd cried so much I didn't think there was anything left in me. My family didn't know I was coming in, and that was only because I couldn't get my voice to sound normal from crying so much. A part of me wanted to turn back around and head back to Charlotte, but the other part knew it was the best decision I could've ever made. Getting the heartbreak over sooner was for the better. Not to mention, I missed Ellie. Seeing her would lessen the pain.

I pulled into the driveway behind my mother's rental car and hopped out. Splashes and screams of joy could be heard out back so I made my way around the house. Ellie and my nieces were in the pool, floating around on inflatable flamingos and kicking water at each other. My mom and my sister were in the gazebo, talking animatedly about something. Probably discussing *Grey's Anatomy* since they loved to watch the seasons over and over.

I watched Ellie for a few minutes, relieved to finally be near her again, but my heart still had a giant hole in it. Would it ever go away? I was afraid of the answer to that question.

Ellie's face lit up when she saw me. "Mommy!"

Kimberly jumped up and took off her sunglasses, staring at me with a concerned look on her face as I walked over to the pool. She knew something was wrong. Ellie scrambled out of the water, and I knelt down to her level. She jumped in my arms with the biggest smile on her face. "You're back! You're back!"

She drenched me, but I didn't care. Tears fell down my cheeks, and I hugged her as tight as I could. "I've missed you so much." Over and over, I kissed her wet cheek. I let her go and held out her arms. "I think you got bigger this summer. I bet you grew two inches."

She perked up. "Good. Maybe this year I'll be taller than the boys."

My mom stood and waved me over. "Hey, sweetheart."

I kissed Ellie again and blew kisses at my nieces. "Go back in. I'll change and play with you in a minute."

When I joined my mom and Kimberly in the gazebo, she hugged me hard. "Why didn't you tell us you were coming in today?"

My eyes burned, but I kept hugging her to keep her from looking at my face. "I wanted to surprise you." I quickly turned to my sister and hugged her, hoping it gave me enough time to calm myself. "Where's Dad?"

"Off fishing. He'll be back in a little bit." She let me go, her brows furrowed as she looked at me. I shook my head, and quickly faced our mother.

"Are you hungry?" my mom asked. "I can go in and heat you up some lasagna. You can eat it out here."

My stomach growled, but I didn't know if I'd be able to eat. My throat felt too thick to be able to swallow anything. I plastered on a smile and nodded. "That'd be great."

Once she was in the house, I sat down across from my sister, who quickly moved her chair closer. "What the hell is going on? I watched Miranda get arrested for breaking into Justin's house. He put a restraining order on her."

With a heavy sigh, I stared off toward the ocean. "She broke in so she could see who I was. She knew Justin was with someone else because a picture of us was leaked. Luckily, you couldn't really see my face."

Kimberly shook her head. "What a psycho."

I scoffed. "You're telling me."

"Are you afraid she'll expose who you are?"

"There's nothing I can do if she does. It was a risk I took being with him," I admitted truthfully. "As long as Ellie's protected, I don't care."

Honestly, I wasn't necessarily afraid of myself being exposed. I cringed at the thought of Miranda spreading lies about me, but on the way here, I realized it didn't matter if our relationship went public. I was proud to be with him for the time I had. All that mattered was that Ellie didn't get brought in it.

"Miranda didn't scare you off, did she?"

"No," I answered, sounding unsure. "I don't know. The crap she said was stuff I already knew. Justin's famous, and I'm a nobody. It would never work."

"How do you know?"

"Seriously?" I huffed, turning to her. "Celebrity relationships don't last long. Just take a look in the tabloids."

She shook her head like she didn't believe a word I said. Hell, deep down I didn't believe it. Justin and I had something real, we just didn't live on the same side of the country.

Kimberly raised her hands in the air and shrugged. "Hey,

from what I know about your relationship, it seemed pretty serious. What did Justin say when you told him you were leaving?"

My chest tightened, and I froze. When I didn't answer, she smacked my arms. "Please tell me you didn't just up and leave behind his back?"

Feeling even more miserable, I nodded. "I freaked out."

Judging by the expression on her face, she disapproved. "I can't believe you left him like that. What's the real reason you left?" My eyes instantly found Ellie, and my chest tightened. Kimberly followed my line of sight and sighed. "Ah, I see. Worried about your little girl?"

"She's everything to me, Kim. What happens if Ellie grows to love Justin, and then one day he says he doesn't want to be with me anymore? Can you imagine how heartbroken she'd be? Not to mention, it'd hurt me twice as much to see in her pain."

Kimberly looked over at our girls swimming in the pool. "There are a lot of ifs there, sis. What you fail to realize is that we have to make ourselves happy as well. If you don't, you'll be miserable for the rest of your life. Have you even talked to him about meeting Ellie?" she asked.

I shook my head. "Doesn't matter. Even if he wanted to meet her, he's not going to be around once hockey starts. What's the point? It'll only confuse her."

She snorted. "Please. Ellie's going to be nine this December. Not to mention, she's smart as hell. Don't underestimate her." Kimberly reached over and grabbed my hand. "Look at me." I did as she said and met her gaze. "Ellie would want you to be happy. If she knew her mother was dating the famous Justin Davis, she'd be over-the-moon excited. The girl wants to be an actress when she grows up."

I rested my head on the table and groaned. "If she only knew how corrupted that lifestyle could be."

"It's a choice she'll have to make on her own when the time comes. You can't protect her forever." She tapped my shoulder, and I lifted my head. "If you really care about Justin, and he about you, you'll make it work. Why don't you call him and be honest with him?"

Our mother walked out the door, carrying a plate of lasagna in one hand and a salad in the other. "I'll think about it," I replied, wishing I had the courage to pick up the phone. I felt horrible for leaving the way I did.

My mother set the food down in front of me and handed me a fork. "Eat up."

Kimberly's phone rang, and she walked away to answer it. I watched her walk around the pool, her face a stony mask as she listened to whoever she was on the phone with. "It's probably Jackson. He's been calling a lot lately. I think he misses her and the girls," my mom said.

I took a bite of the lasagna. "About damn time."

My mother rubbed my shoulder. "I keep praying you find someone like Trey again. He was a good man."

The lump in my throat was back. I'd already found someone, but I let him go. "I do too, Momma. I do too."

It was getting late, but I didn't want to close my eyes just yet. My parents sat at the kitchen table, playing cards, while I stood by the patio door, watching the moon's reflection in the ocean. I didn't want to go to sleep after the day I had. Justin would no doubt be all I'd dream about.

"Meghan, why don't you come play cards with us?"

I took one last look at the dark ocean water and sat down at the table with them. My father handed me the deck, and I cut it so he could finish shuffling. "What are we playing?" I asked, knowing full well what he wanted to play. It was his favorite game.

Grinning wide, he dealt the cards. "Kings in the corner."

Kimberly was on the couch reading, but she kept looking down at her phone. "Want to play?" I called out.

She shook her head. "I'm waiting on a phone call."

And just then, her phone rang, and she jumped off the couch. She smiled and hurried down the stairs to the main level of the house. My parents had designed the three-level house to have the master bedroom, living room, and kitchen on the top floor. The middle floor was all bedrooms, and the lower level had more bedrooms and the game room. It was huge. When they'd had it built, they'd hoped they'd have a lot more grandchildren to occupy the rooms.

My father gently touched my wrist. "Pumpkin, you okay?"

It took me a few seconds to focus on what he said. "Yeah, I'm fine. Just thinking."

His brows furrowed. "About what? You look sad." My mother agreed with a nod.

I opened my mouth to speak, but nothing came out. Kimberly's footsteps thumped on the stairs, and she came back into the room, biting her lip nervously. She held out her hand to someone I couldn't see, and I figured it'd be Jackson, but the person who turned the corner wasn't him at all.

"Justin," I choked.

Kimberly let his hand go and nudged him toward us. There was sadness all over his face, no smile to be seen. I wasn't used to seeing hm so upset. Maybe he felt just as horrible as I did. Justin walked over and held a hand out to my father. "Hi, sir. My name's Justin."

Kimberly cut in and waved a hand between my parents. "Justin, these are our parents, Roger and Denise."

Mouth gaping, my mother fanned herself so fast I could barely see her hands. My father looked over at her like she'd lost her mind. "What are you doing?" he asked her.

She stood and rushed over to Justin, taking his hand away from my father, and shaking it excitedly. "I don't know why you're here, but this is the best early birthday present ever."

My father looked lost, and turned to me. "Do you know what's going on?"

Trying my best to keep the tears at bay, I nodded. "He's Justin Davis, Dad. Center forward for the Charlotte Strikers, and last season's bachelor on the *Rich and Single*. You've seen him on TV before."

It was his turn to be shocked. "Oh." His eyes widened, and he gasped. "Oh, that guy." He stood quickly and shook Justin's hand. "Sorry, son. I'm more of a golf man, not hockey."

Justin let his hand go, and tried his best to smile. "So I've heard. Meghan told me you loved golf."

I waited for my parents to ask why he was there, and that did it. They both turned to me, their faces full of surprise. My mother broke from the trance, and glanced back and forth between me and Justin. "Sorry, but how do you two know each other?"

Justin waited on me to answer. My heart pounded so hard and fast, it started to hurt. "It's actually a funny story," I began, "but to sum it all up, Justin and I have been seeing each other the past few weeks. He bought the Southfork Ranch. It's because of him I was able to get the fence and barn done at home."

The room fell silent. They could obviously tell there was some tension between us. Kimberly reached for their hands and pulled them away. "Why don't we let Justin and Meghan talk before you ask more questions."

Both my parents seemed to still be in shock, but they backed away. Kimberly nodded toward the stairs, and I took Justin's hand. "Let's go take a walk."

Justin gripped onto my hand, and it only broke my heart more. I'd only been away from him for several hours, and I missed his touch. How was I ever going to let him go again? We quietly made it down the stairs to the bottom floor and out the back door to the wooden walkway. It led right down to the beach, where the waves crashed against the shore. As soon as we hit the sand, he pulled me into his arms.

"Holy fuck, angel. I thought maybe I'd never get to hold you like this again."

Tears streamed down my cheeks. "I didn't want to leave you," I cried. "I felt like I had no choice." He held me so tight that I couldn't move. I didn't want to. I wanted him to hold me for as long as he could. Voice shaking, I buried my head against his chest. "I'm so sorry."

"I'm sorry too, for not keeping you safe in my own home. You have to believe that my life isn't crazy like that all the time."

He let me go, and I stared up at him. There were tears in his eyes, and it broke my heart. "How did you find me?"

His fingers caressed my cheek. "I figured you'd come to Nags Head. I just didn't know what house. My private investigator found you and gave me your sister's number."

Gasping, I stepped back. "She knew you were coming?"

He nodded. "I was going to anyway, but I knew she was aware of our relationship. I had to make sure I was welcome here first. And," he began with a sigh, "I wanted to come at a time I knew Ellie would be in bed. That way, if you don't want me here, you don't run the risk of her seeing me."

"Justin, I—"

He placed a finger on my lips. "Wait. Before you tell me to

go, you need to hear this." Sliding his hands up arms, he brought them to my face and cupped my cheeks. "I know you're afraid of me meeting Ellie. Callie told me what you said about if I were to ever leave you, I wouldn't only be breaking your heart, but Ellie's as well." He stepped closer, his body melded against mine. "I'm here to tell you that's not going to happen."

I shook my head. "How do you know that?"

His lips closed over mine, and I shut my eyes, enjoying the feel of him. My heart was so full it felt like it was going to explode. After we broke from the kiss, he rested his forehead to mine. "I love you, Meghan. That's how I know I won't break your heart."

The breath whooshed out of my lungs, and I gasped. "What?"

A sad smile spread across his face. "I said, I love you."

It was all I wanted to hear from the very beginning. Lips trembling, I covered his hands with mine and squeezed. "I love you too. So much it hurts."

He kissed me again, this time more urgent than before. "Do you have any idea how much I've wanted to hear you say that?"

We kissed again, and I smiled as the tears came tumbling down. "Just as much as I wanted to hear it from you."

"I want to be a part of your life *and* Ellie's. If you don't want that, I'll go. I understand if you don't think I'll be a good father figure, but I want you more than I've wanted anything in this world. I'll do whatever it takes to make you happy and to keep you with me."

He wiped the tears off my face, and I shook my head. "We have two weeks, Justin. After that, you go back to your life, and I go back to mine. How will it ever work?"

Eyes full of raw heat, he held me tighter. "We'll make it work. But in order to do that, you have to be willing to *be* with me. No secrets. No hiding out from the press. I know you want to stay hidden, but in reality, that won't last long."

"It's okay," I murmured truthfully. "I'm fine with people knowing who I am. I just want Ellie to be protected."

"I'll protect her with everything I have. All I'm asking for is a chance. Don't push me away."

Taking a deep breath, I let it out slow. I didn't even have to think twice. I knew what my heart wanted, and I was a fool for trying to deny it. "All right," I said. "I'm willing to make this work."

Chuckling, Justin picked me up and swung me around. "This makes me so damn happy."

"Hey, you still have to meet Ellie. If she doesn't like you, all deals are off."

His eyes twinkled. "Oh, she's going to love me. I'll make sure of it."

Wrapping my arms around his neck, I smiled up at him. "One more thing."

"What?" he said, holding me around the waist.

"What are we going to say to Ellie if she asks if you're my boyfriend?"

That dashing smile of his was back. "We tell her yes. I'm yours, and you're mine. And in another sense, I'm hers too … if she wants me."

"She'll love you, just like I do."

Justin glanced back at the house, and then out at the ocean. "Want to take a walk?"

I shook my head, and slowly slid my hand down his shorts. "Actually, I have a better idea."

His cock twitched and hardened in my grasp. "I'm all up for that."

CHAPTER TWENTY-THREE

JUSTIN

By the time we'd gotten back to the house last night, everyone had gone to sleep. I made sure to leave Meghan's bed early in case Ellie decided to crawl in with her like Meghan said she was known to do. I had to admit, I was nervous as hell to meet her. What if she didn't like me? My relationship with Meghan depended on mine and Ellie's.

Everything was quiet in the house. The sun hadn't even risen yet. I sat on the edge of the couch, watching the sky slowly lighten over the horizon. The door to the master bedroom opened, and Meghan's father walked out, wearing a pair of plaid pajama pants and a white T-shirt. He saw me and waved.

"Good morning."

"Good morning," I replied back. "I made coffee."

Roger smiled and gave a thumbs-up. "You're the man." He

poured a cup of coffee, and came over next to me. "Did you and Meghan work things out?"

"I hope so. She's letting me meet Ellie today. I'm not going to lie, I'm nervous. I want her to like me."

Roger slapped a hand down on my shoulder. "Just be yourself and you have nothing to worry about. Although I did hear some not-so-good stuff about you last night. Makes me worry for my daughter."

I stood and faced him so he could see how serious I was. "I know. We all make mistakes, and I've made plenty of them. I love your daughter. I'll do anything to make her happy."

He studied me for a second, and then smiled. "I know. I figured that out last night when you came all the way out here." Footsteps sounded on the stairs, and we both looked to see who it was.

With her hair in a messy ponytail and wearing her pink pajamas, Meghan waved at us. "Good morning."

Her father squeezed my shoulder. "Good luck today." He walked toward Meghan and kissed her on the cheek, whispering something in her ear that made her smile.

She opened her arms and wrapped them around my waist. "You ready for this?"

My pulse had been racing all morning. "Of course. Not nervous at all."

Lifting her brows, I could tell she didn't believe me. "You'll be fine. Ellie's probably going to be really excited when she realizes who you are."

"That's not the only reason she'll like me, is it?"

Meghan leaned up on her toes and kissed me. "Just be your charming self. She's never seen me with a man before, other than her Paw Paw and Uncle Emmett, so I have no clue how she's going to take it. We'll spend time with her today, just you, me, and her."

"That sounds like a good plan," her mother said, coming out of the bedroom in her light blue robe.

Meghan shook her head and put a hand over her mouth to hide her smile. "Mom, what are you doing? You never have your hair and makeup done this early in the morning."

Her mother lightly touched her hair and shrugged. "What? There's a famous actor and pro athlete in the house."

Meghan patted my arm. "Don't worry, he's used to seeing the unglamorous side to me."

I kissed the top of her head. "And I love it."

"Awe, that's so sweet," her mother gushed, waving her hand toward the kitchen table. "Sit down and tell me how you two met."

Meghan snickered and pulled me over to the table. "It's really funny, actually. It was the day I came home. I literally walked into Justin and recognized him immediately." She looked over at me. "The second I saw his eyes, there was no mistaking it. Anyway," she said, turning back to her mother. "I pretended not to know who he was. He needed a ride, so I took him home."

I reached over and squeezed her hand. "I had no clue she knew who I was. I thought it was nice being able to be around someone who didn't. I offered to fix the fence and the barn just to be with her."

Her mother placed a hand over her chest. "That is so sweet. So you're the one who fixed the fence?"

I nodded. "We both did. Meghan helped."

"And once that was done," Meghan began, "he brought me to North Carolina to meet some of his family."

I'd noticed her father paying attention to everything we said while he poured his coffee. "I guess you two are pretty serious then?" he asked.

Looking over at Meghan, I brought her hand up to my lips and kissed it. "We are. I love her."

Her father came over to the table and glanced at us both before settling his gaze on mine. "I can see when a man realizes what's in front of him. You came all the way out here to take a chance with my daughter. I wish Kim's husband was smart enough to see what he has instead of working all the damn time. There's nothing more precious than time with your family." He set his coffee cup down on the table, and turned a sad smile to Meghan. "If he's what you want, I support you. I'm just curious how you're going to be together when you live in Wyoming, and he's based in North Carolina."

Meghan sighed, and she looked at me. "We haven't worked that out yet."

"But we will," I added. "We'll figure it out."

Light footsteps echoed from the hallway downstairs. Meghan grabbed my arm and squeezed. "Ellie's awake."

Everything moved in slow motion. When Ellie turned the corner in matching pink pajamas like Meghan's, and her dark hair in messy curls, she looked exactly like a mini version of her mother. Ellie rubbed her eyes and yawned as she slowly walked over to us, keeping her head down as if she was going to fall back asleep.

"You guys woke me up with all your talking."

"You needed to get up anyway," Meghan said. She leaned in close to me. "She can be sassy. Just forewarning you."

"I think I can handle it."

Meghan got up and picked Ellie up in her arms. Ellie laid her head down on her shoulder and closed her eyes. "Ellie-Bear, we have a guest. He'll be staying with us the next two weeks."

Ellie slowly opened her eyes, and that was when she finally saw me. She blinked a couple of times and stared at me, her brows furrowed in confusion. "Haven't I seen him before?" she asked, her voice just above a whisper.

Meghan giggled and kissed her cheek. "Yeah. You've seen him on TV. His name's Justin Davis."

I waved. "Hey, Ellie."

"Oh, my God," she squealed, jumping out of Meghan's arms. Eyes as wide as could be, she stared transfixed at me. "I can't wait to tell my friends at school."

Meghan bit her lip and shrugged. "Guess there's no keeping a secret now." She gently pushed Ellie toward me. "Why don't you introduce yourself?" I slid out of the chair and down to my knees so I could be on her level.

Ellie squealed again and rushed over to me. She definitely wasn't shy. "I'm Ellie," she said, holding out her little hand and doing a small dance of excitement.

She had a firm grip when I shook it; I was impressed. "Justin. It's nice to meet you, Ellie. Your mother told me a lot about you."

Still shaking my hand, she looked back at Meghan, and then back to me. "Are you my mom's boyfriend?"

Meghan snorted, and nodded for me to answer. "I am. Is that okay with you?"

All my reservations were put at ease when she flung her tiny arms around my neck. Her laugh was the cutest sound I'd ever heard. "Yes!" she squealed.

I hugged her back, and peered up at Meghan with the biggest grin on my face. "Ellie, how would you like to spend the day out on the beach with me and your mom? I'd like to get to know you better."

She let me go, and jumped up and down. "Let me get my bathing suit on." She ran to the stairs, giggling the whole way.

I stood, and Meghan nodded. "I think we're off to a good start."

I sure as hell hoped so.

CHAPTER TWENTY-FOUR

MEGHAN

I WAS AMAZED AT HOW well Ellie attached to Justin. Maybe it was because she was starstruck, although I wanted to believe it was because Justin was being so sweet to her. "Mommy, watch this!" Ellie shouted.

She was out in the ocean with Justin, waiting on the perfect wave. He had her on the boogie board, ready to let her go. That was all they'd done for the past two hours, while I sat on my beach towel and watched them. Justin waved at me to catch my attention. "This one's it!"

A wave came up behind him, and he pushed the boogie board forward. Ellie screamed and laughed as she sailed across the water to the shore. Justin ran toward her so he could help her up. My cheeks hurt from smiling so much. The level of excitement on Ellie's face was something I'd never seen before. Even Justin surprised me. With Ellie, he acted like a big kid; it was sweet, and something I didn't expect.

Ellie ran up to me with Justin behind her, pulling the boogie board behind him. She plopped down in front of me, spraying me with droplets of ocean water. "Justin said he's going to take us for ice cream later."

"He did, did he?" I asked, grinning at Justin.

He sat down beside me and shrugged. "Hey, you can't spend a day out in this hot sun without getting some ice cream."

I looked around at the other people on the beach. No one seemed to realize they were in the midst of a star. If we went to a public place, our chances of anonymity would go down drastically.

"Are you sure that's a good idea?" I asked.

Justin and Ellie's smiles both faded. Ellie cocked her head to the side. "Why wouldn't it be? It's just ice cream."

"I know that, honey. Justin is a well-known person. If someone recognizes him, they'll post pictures, and the next thing you know the paparazzi will be here camping out in our yard. The whole reason I was scared to let you meet Justin was because of that. As soon as the paparazzi know who we are, privacy will be hard to come by."

Justin sat down beside her. "Your mom's right. Maybe we should keep this place a secret. That way, the paparazzi can't ruin it for us."

Ellie fiddled with a handful of sand and sighed. "Do we have to stay hidden forever? That doesn't sound like fun. I want to be famous too."

I should've known Ellie would want to be in the spotlight. Justin tried his best to hide his smile, and failed miserably. "Sorry," he whispered, "that was funny."

Rolling my eyes, I tapped Ellie's chin. "We're not going to stay hidden forever. But like Justin said, maybe it's best to keep this place a secret. That way, we can come back here and know that we have our privacy."

Ellie nodded. "Okay. But when can Justin take us places? No one at school will believe me when I tell them."

Justin sighed, but I could see the mischief in his eyes. "She has a point. I, for one, would love to show off you beautiful ladies to the world. Maybe even get this little one," he said, poking Ellie playfully in the side, "an acting gig. You do want to be an actress, don't you?"

Ellie jumped to her feet, and danced around. "Oh, my goodness, yes! Can you do that?"

Justin winked at her. "I can do anything. That is, if your mom's okay with it?"

Ellie clasped her hands together, and gave me her puppy-dog face. "Please, Mommy. It's all I want."

I had my reservations, but I had to trust that Justin knew what he was doing. "Okay," I gave in. "I'm fine with it. Justin and I haven't discussed the future yet, but I know he has to be back in Charlotte in a couple of weeks to start hockey practice. We could possibly visit him the weekend before school starts?"

The look on Justin's face made my heart melt. I knew he was waiting on me to make the first step. Ellie jumped in my arms. "Can we? Can we? I love riding in planes."

"How about a private jet?" Justin asked. "I can have it ready for you at the airport."

Ellie squealed and danced around, her hands going ninety miles as she waved them in the air. "Oh, my gosh, I can't believe this! I have to tell Maw Maw and Paw Paw."

She ran toward the house, screaming for my parents. Justin roared with laughter and laid down on the towel next to me. "That girl is after my heart. She's just like you, only she wants to be famous and you don't."

I laid down beside him. "She has no clue what your world is like, Justin. All I want is to make the right decisions for her, and myself."

"It's not as bad as you think, angel. Yes, the paparazzi can be a pain in the fucking ass, but you have to think of all the people out there that deal with it. My sister and Dallas, Lacey, and Maddox. They have a baby, and they're doing fine. Pictures of them do get published from time to time, but it's all because people love seeing them together." He sat up, and looked down at me. "You and I can be the same way. Ellie can have everything she's ever dreamed of."

I reached up and cupped his cheek. "You make it sound so easy."

"It is easy. We can do this." He leaned down and kissed me. "It's time, angel. I want everyone to know you're mine."

Taking a deep breath, I sat up and shook my head. "I can't believe I'm doing this. Nothing will ever be the same."

Justin chuckled. "No, but it'll be worth it."

CHAPTER TWENTY-FIVE

MEGHAN

THE FIRST WEEK PASSED BY in a blur. Every day, Justin and I spent time with Ellie, and they grew closer and closer. He was determined to take her to her favorite ice cream shop, and ended up calling the manager to see if we could have a private session after hours. He paid a nice chunk of change for that private time, but it was a treat for my family. Everyone went.

Ellie and my nieces giggled and screamed as Justin tossed them this way and that in the pool. My father even joined in, and it was the girls against the guys. My mom watched them and laughed. “He’s so good with the kids. Your father has thoroughly enjoyed his company. They stayed up all last night talking about golf.”

Grinning, I grabbed a strawberry off the fruit tray and took a bite. “Yes, I know. I fell asleep listening to them. Golf is boring, even to talk about.”

Kimberly walked out of the house carrying a plate with my mom's leftover chocolate birthday cake. She set it down in front of us, and we all grabbed a fork. Justin had heard her talk about this fancy curio cabinet she wanted, so he ordered it, and it was going to be shipped to their house when they got back to Wyoming. He was trying hard to make a good impression, but I didn't want him to feel like he had to do all those grand things to be accepted by my family.

"Have you figured out the game plan for when he leaves next week?" Kimberly asked.

I kept my focus on Justin and Ellie. "For the most part. Ellie and I are going to fly out and see him the weekend before school starts. After that, we're going to play it by ear. Justin says he'll come out to Wyoming every chance he gets. Until games start, we'll have every weekend." Which I knew wasn't going to be much. "Then, after that, he said he'll fly us to his games."

"That's a busy lifestyle, sis. Think you can handle it?"

"Yes," I said without hesitation. I looked over at her and nodded. "I think it'll be an adventure."

Her lips pulled back into a smile. "That's what I wanted to hear. He's a good guy, Meghan. I want it to work out between you two."

My mother rubbed my shoulder. "Me too, sweetheart. And not because he bought me that expensive curio cabinet I wanted either. He's genuinely a good person." Her gaze landed on him in the pool. "Just look at him with the girls. He'll make a wonderful father."

I rolled my eyes. "You're getting ahead of yourself, Mom. We haven't even talked about marriage."

Kimberly winked. "Not yet anyway. It will one day though. The guy's head over heels for you." Her smile slightly faded, and she sighed. "I'd love it if my husband made half the effort

Justin has for us. I haven't been able to get in touch with him today."

Jackson worked a lot, and it was hard for him to take time off. I know Kimberly missed him. She focused on the cake, and picked at it. At least until my mother gasped, and accidentally smacked the fork out of her hand trying to get her attention. "Mom, what are you doing?" she snapped.

She pointed at the house, and walking out of the back door was Jackson. Kimberly slapped a hand to her mouth and gasped. Her girls screamed, and jumped out of the pool to hug their dad, their cries of excitement filling the air. Kimberly ran over to them, and joined in on the family embrace.

Justin and Ellie walked over, and I couldn't help but notice the devilish smile on Justin's face. "Why do you look like that?" I asked.

He shrugged, and glanced back at Kimberly and Jackson. "No reason."

Then it hit me. Over the past couple of days, he'd asked Kimberly a lot of questions about Jackson and where he worked. He'd taken a huge interest in their relationship. "What did you do?"

He held up his hands. "Nothing. Want to take a walk with me and Ellie?"

Gaze narrowed, I ate a bite of the chocolate cake. "You can't fool me."

Mom giggled and slapped my back. "Have fun on your walk."

I took Ellie's hand and she grabbed onto Justin's. We swung her in the air, and she giggled. It felt so normal, like we were a family. Once we were on the sand, I stared at Justin, pursing my lips. "What did you do to Jackson?"

Ellie snickered, and my attention snapped to her. She looked up at Justin, and he shook his head, like there was a secret between them. "Seriously? My daughter knows what you're up to, and I don't?"

Ellie giggled again. "It was a secret, Mommy. I told Justin I wouldn't tell."

Justin stopped and knelt down in front of her, both of them trying to contain their mischief. "All right, peanut, I think it's time I tell Mommy what I did. I don't want her getting mad at us."

Ellie nodded. "Okay."

Justin stood, and bit his lip. "I kind of called Jackson, and persuaded him to come down here. I told him that Kimberly and the girls missed him."

"How did he get the time off of work? His company never approves anything."

His grin widened. "Power of persuasion, I guess."

Ellie tapped her foot on the sand. "That's not what it was."

Justin hung his head and laughed. "Fine. I bribed Jackson's boss with season tickets to watch his favorite football team."

The look on Kimberly's face when Jackson showed up was priceless. She was so happy. I didn't care what Justin had to do to get Jackson here, as long as it brought him back to Kimberly and his girls.

"Thanks, Justin. You have no idea how happy it made Kimberly."

He shrugged. "Glad to help. I really like your family, Meghan. They make me feel like I'm a part of it."

"You are!" Ellie called out.

Justin knelt back down. "I am, huh? Sure you don't want to trade me in for someone else?"

Ellie shook her head. "Nope. You make my mom happy. She hasn't been that way in a long time."

Justin looked up at me and sighed. "I'm hoping I can make her happy for a very long time. And you too," he said, tapping her nose. "You've kind of grown on me."

Ellie hooked her arms around his neck. "I like you too."

It was in that moment, I realized everything was going to be okay.

CHAPTER TWENTY-SIX

JUSTIN

The house was quiet, and it was the first night I hadn't talked to Meghan's father till early hours in the morning. We had so many things in common. I knew it drove Meghan insane. She walked across the hall to check on Ellie, and then quietly snuck back into the bedroom, locking the door behind her.

"It's about time I get you to myself. I was starting to get jealous of my dad."

I patted the bed. "Hey, I can't help it. He's an interesting man. I told him I was going to introduce him to Lucas Montgomery. I think that sealed the deal with him liking me."

She curled up beside me. "He likes you no matter what. You don't have to bribe my family to get them to like you."

I shrugged. "I'm not. I enjoy doing things for your family. They actually appreciate it."

Meghan smiled. "That they do. I appreciate it too. I just wish I knew of a way to pay you back."

So many things ran through my mind; my dick twitched just thinking about it. "I'm sure I can think up a few ways." She bit her lip and leaned in to kiss me. Before she could, Ellie's voice echoed from across the hall.

"Mommy!" Her voice sounded sad and scared.

Meghan kissed me quick, and slid off the bed. "Hold that thought—I'll be right back."

"Wait. Let me go." She stood by the door, and I joined her. "I want to see if I can help her on my own."

Meghan opened the door, and nodded. "Go. Holler for me if you need me."

Ellie called out her mother's name again, and I slowly tiptoed into the room so I wouldn't wake up her two cousins who were on the bunk bed across the room. Ellie sat up in bed, clutching her pink teddy bear.

"Hey," I whispered, "you okay?"

Sniffling, she shook her head. "I had a nightmare."

I knelt down beside her bed. "I'm sorry, peanut. Do you want to talk about it?"

She laid back down. "It was scary. Mommy and I were in the woods, and a snake bit her. I thought she was going to die."

"That's not going to happen," I assured her. "Do you want me to get her?"

"No, it's okay. I'm fine now. But if you want, you can talk to me for a few minutes so I don't fall asleep back to that dream." With her amber, puppy-dog eyes and innocent smile, there was no way I'd ever be able to refuse her. She moved over on the bed so I could sit down beside her.

"What do you want to talk about?" I asked, keeping my voice low.

She shrugged. "Anything. Are you excited to play hockey again?"

"More than excited. I miss the ice."

"My favorite movie is *Ice Princess*. It's about a figure skater. Mommy never had the money to get me ice skating lessons."

My chest tightened, but it also made me excited to know I could do it for her. "You don't need lessons when you have me. I can teach you how to skate. Then, when you get good at the basics, I can get you private figure skating lessons."

Her face lit up. "Really?"

"Of course. There's nothing I wouldn't do for you." I tucked her bear underneath her covers. "What else would you want? Give me a list."

She pursed her little lips, and looked up at the ceiling as if she was deep in thought. "Let's see. You've already taken care of the most important thing, and that was to make my mommy be happy again. I know she's going to be sad when you have to go back home."

"I know, peanut. I'm going to be sad too, but I told her I'm going to fly out and see you both as much as I can. In fact, I have a surprise for you both when you get back to Wyoming."

"You do?" she gasped. "What is it?"

"Can you keep a secret?"

She nodded quickly, and held out her pinky. "I pinky promise." We linked fingers, and I whispered the secret in her ear. "Oh, my goodness. She's going to be so happy."

"That's what I was hoping for." She let my finger go, and sunk further into the covers. I kissed her forehead, and tucked her in. "Are you okay now?"

Yawning, she held her bear close. "Yes." I got up, and slowly walked back to the door. "Justin?"

I turned around. "Yeah?"

She lifted her head slightly over the pillow so she could see me. "Is this what having a father is like?"

So many emotions hit me like a ton of bricks. I never thought I could have so much love for a child that wasn't my own. I'd only spent a week with her, and she had me wrapped around her little fingers. And my heart was breaking for her, too, that she'd never known the kind of love a father had for a daughter. I walked back over to her, and knelt back down.

"Yes," I murmured. "If your father was alive, I know he'd come running every time you called his name. From what your mother told me, he was an amazing man. I'm sorry you never got to know him."

Her eyes glistened. "Mommy lets me watch their wedding video so I can see him. All of my friends have fathers, and I've always wondered what it would be like. You'd be a good one."

I ruffled her dark hair. "Thanks, peanut. That means a lot to me." I tucked her in one last time, and she closed her eyes. When I got back to the bedroom, Meghan had already fallen asleep. I tried not to wake her, but the bed jostled her when I slid in.

"Everything okay?" she asked, snuggling up against me.

I wrapped my arm around her and rubbed her shoulder. "She's fine. We had a heart to heart."

"Oh yeah? What about?"

"That's between me and Ellie," I teased. She slapped my stomach, and I laughed. "So listen, next week is our last week together. I thought maybe we could spend a couple of those days doing what we were supposed to for my birthday."

She gasped and sat up. "The private island?"

I nodded. "I thought it'd be nice to have just a little bit of time to ourselves. Then we can come back here, and I'll have the private jet for you and your family to take back home."

Sighing, she sat up. "Justin, you don't have to do that. I don't want you spending your money on me and my family."

Taking her face in my hands, I kissed her long and hard. "I

love you, angel. I've said this before—there's nothing I wouldn't do for you."

A tear slid down her cheek. "Same goes for you. I love you so much."

I rolled on top of her, and winked. "Then show me."

CHAPTER TWENTY-SEVEN

MEGHAN

THE LAST WEEK MOVED BY quickly, leaving Justin and I only one night on his friend's private island. Neither Justin nor I minded because it was time we got to spend together with Ellie. That was the most important thing to me right now, getting them a solid relationship started before we had to separate ways.

Justin reached over and grabbed my hand, drawing me away from the scenic view of the ocean below. "We're almost there," he said, his voice echoing from the headset.

I thought we were going to get to the island by boat, but Justin surprised me with a helicopter ride. I'd never been on one before, and I wasn't going to lie ... it kind of scared me. Thoughts of crashing into the water and getting eaten by a shark passed through my mind a time or two.

Justin glanced out the window, and squeezed my hand. "There it is." He pointed to the island, and I breathed a sigh of relief. It was covered in trees, but I could see the roof of the cottage.

"Where do we land?" I asked, hoping it didn't have to be in the water. I wasn't scared to swim, just terrified of the creatures lurking beneath.

The pilot, whose name was Charles Patterson, glanced back at us. "Mr. Montgomery had a helicopter pad built on the front side of the island. You'll see it when we get closer. He did it for his guests who don't like boats. That way they have another option."

He flew us around the island so we could see all of it, and then landed us on the front side by the dock. There were two kayaks floating to the side of it, along with a wooden boat and paddles. It was strange to think that the whole island was ours until tomorrow.

Charles took off his headset and slipped out of the helicopter. He came over to my side and opened the door. Once we were out, Charles shook Justin's hand. "I'll be back tomorrow at noon," he shouted, his voice barely audible over the helicopter blades.

Justin and I hurried over to the other side of the dock while Charles lifted the helicopter into the air and flew away. It was a little scary to know we were on the island by ourselves, with no one around to help if something happened, but it was also exhilarating.

Taking a deep breath, I glanced around, trying to soak it all in. "I can't believe this is real."

Justin grinned. "And it's all ours. Just the first of many places we'll get to see together. Ellie's going to love it. We can take her to Disney World, Paris, Alaska—anywhere you both want to go."

It was like a dream come true. Wrapping my arms around his waist, I looked up at him. "You don't have to take me places to make me happy."

He kissed the tip of my nose. "I know. I'm doing it because I want to. You told me a few nights ago that you've barely been anywhere besides Wyoming and North Carolina. I want to change that."

I shrugged. "Hey, if that's what you want to do, I can't complain. It all just feels like I'm in a dream, and I keep expecting to wake up."

"No dream, angel. This is all real." He flung our bag over his shoulder, and turned to the white sandy path that was lined with palm trees. "How about we drop our bag off and explore before it gets too dark?"

"Sounds good to me."

We walked up the path and through the trees until we arrived at the teal-colored cottage with a light gray tin roof. It was up on stilts, so we had to climb a lot of stairs to get inside. When we opened the door, it was magical. There were fresh flowers on the kitchen table, and the whole place was bright and open.

Justin set our bag down on the floor, and grabbed my hand. "Let's go. I want to see this place." He pulled me along, and I giggled at how excited he was. There was a path that led to the back side of the island, and that was where he took me. "Lucas said the waves are awesome on the back side, and that you'll love all the seashells. I think his wife found an eight-inch conch shell."

"That's pretty big," I said, enjoying the hike through the trees.

When the trees opened up to the beach, he was right. The waves crashed against the shore, and there were all sorts of things on the sand. Seashells of all sizes and colors were everywhere. We walked over to the water's edge, and my feet slowly sunk in the wet sand. Gazing out at the water, there was nothing but miles and miles of ocean.

We stood there for a few minutes – hand in hand – until

Justin's sigh broke the silence. "We go our separate ways tomorrow."

My chest tightened. "I know. I'm not ready to say goodbye, but we have to." I'd been trying to forget about it, but there was no escaping it. I turned to face him, and I could see the turmoil in his eyes. "What if the distance becomes too much?"

He shook his head. "I'm not going to let that happen. No matter what happens, we're going to make this work. I need to hear you say it too."

Taking his other hand, I pulled him closer. "No matter what happens, we're going to make this work. I just wish I wasn't so scared to let you go. I'm afraid I'll never see you again."

He leaned down, and kissed me. "You'll be surprised how much you see me. Flying to Wyoming is a piece of cake."

But how long was he going to do that before he got tired of it? That was the big question, and one I didn't want to ask. I had to think positive. "Okay," I said, pulling him down the beach. We slowly walked along the water line, and I picked up shells. Justin gazed out at the ocean, and his focus landed on something in the water. "What do you see?" I asked, curious.

The waves brought it closer, but he had to go in a little way to pick it up. It was just a clear glass bottle, but as he brought it closer, there was something inside of it. Justin held it up and smiled. "Looks like a message in a bottle."

I gasped with excitement; it was so cool to find something like that. Justin brought it over, and we knelt down in the sand. There was a cork in the top, with a folded, light pink piece of paper inside, along with a dried piece of what appeared to be lavender.

Justin pried the cork out, and it took a little bit of maneuvering to get to the piece of paper. He handed it to me, and I opened it gently.

I read the message out loud.

Always follow your dreams, but don't leave the ones you love behind. You might come to find it's too late if you do.

"Sounds kind of sad," I said, rolling the paper up. "Hopefully, whoever wrote it wasn't too late."

Justin pulled out his phone, and took a picture of the note. "Maybe we can find out. If this note goes viral, the person who wrote it might see it and contact us." Justin slipped it back into the bottle, and pushed the cork in.

It made me wonder what kind of person wrote it. Judging by the handwriting and the lavender, I'd say it was a woman. "Hopefully, whoever it was got their happily ever after. In this day and time, it's hard to find that."

Justin put his arm around my shoulders, and squeezed me tight. "We may not have ours just yet, but in time, we will."

I wanted to believe he was right.

THE DAY PASSED BY WAY too quickly, just like every other day I'd spent with Justin. To save us trouble, Lucas had a chef-prepared meal in the refrigerator so all we had to do was heat it up. It was perfect.

Justin had disappeared off into the bedroom, and I took a seat on the couch. It was closing in on ten o'clock, and I dreaded going to sleep. I didn't want to waste time with Justin by sleeping. Brows furrowed, I could hear him fumbling around in the bedroom, but I couldn't see what he was doing.

"Justin?" The door opened, and he came out with a large blanket and a battery-powered lantern. "What is that for?"

He winked. "Come and see. It's a surprise."

I followed him out the door, and we walked all the way down to the calm side of the island. The sand was softer, almost like clay. Justin turned off the lantern, and spread out the blanket.

"Do you know what tonight is?" he asked, lying down on the blanket.

I shook my head and dropped down beside him. "What's tonight?"

Hands tucked behind his head, he stared up at the sky. "Tonight is the peak night to see the Perseid Meteor shower."

Excitement bubbled in my chest. I'd totally forgotten about that. The Perseid Meteor shower always occurred between mid-July to the end of August. I stared up at the sky and waited. So far from inhabited land, we'd no doubt be able to see a ton of the meteors. That was one of the reasons why I loved living in Wyoming. You could see the stars as if they were close enough to touch.

"Let's make a bet," Justin said.

"A bet? For what?" I looked over at his mischievous grin.

He nodded toward the sky. "To see who can find the most meteors. I bet I'll see more of them."

"What do I get if I win?"

His gaze met mine, and there was a seriousness there that made me shiver. "You can ask me any question you want, and I'll answer with full honesty. If I win, it applies to you as well."

I shook his hand. "Deal."

There were so many questions that rolled through my mind, but I had no clue what to even ask if I won. Lying back on the blanket, I concentrated on the sky.

"Found one," Justin called out, pointing at the sky. I'd caught the tail end of the meteor as it fizzled out. A few seconds later, he pointed again. "Found another."

I flung my arm over, and smacked his stomach. "What the hell? You must really want to ask me something."

"You have no idea." About twenty minutes passed by, and he had found a total of four, while I only saw two. Turning his body to me, he took a deep breath and let it out slow. It was almost like he was nervous. Justin was never nervous around me.

"Hey," I said, running a hand through his hair. "What's going on? Why couldn't you just ask me the question without having to win the right?"

He shrugged. "By winning, it gives me an official reason."

Now I was nervous. "Ask me?"

Reaching over, he grabbed my hand and brought it to his lips. He stared at my hand for a few seconds before meeting my eyes again. "What would you say if…"

I waited for him to continue, but all he did was stare at me. "If what?" I asked.

"What would you say if I asked to be traded to Colorado? That way, I could be closer to you. I would do Wyoming if they actually had a major team." That was not what I expected him to ask. Mouth gaping, I stared at him like he'd lost his mind. There were no words. "Why are you looking at me like that?"

"Because I'm wondering if you're serious?"

He nodded. "I am. I was hoping you'd have a happier response."

My eyes burned, and a tear fell down my cheek. Nothing would make me happier than to have him closer to me and Ellie. Only it wasn't going to work. "I can't let you do that, Justin."

"Why not?" He sat up, and I could see the hurt on his face.

"Because," I said, wiping my tears away, "the Charlotte Strikers is where you belong. You have family in North Carolina. I don't want you leaving it all for me."

"I don't understand."

Lifting my hands, I cupped his cheeks, hoping like hell he

could see how much it hurt me to turn him down. "I don't know what our future holds, but I do know that I love you. If I thought you moving to Colorado was a good decision, I'd feel it in my soul. What if in the next couple of months, we don't work out?"

"We will," he countered.

I shook my head. "I'm not going to have you resent me for uprooting yourself when you clearly belonged somewhere else. Hockey is your first love. I saw your face the second you stepped on the ice the other week. I refuse to come between that." Moving closer, I rested my forehead to his. "Promise me you'll stay where you're at."

When he didn't answer, I sat back, and he turned his head, his jaw muscles clenching. "I promise."

I kissed his cheek, and laid my head on his shoulder. "Thank you," I murmured. "You have to know how hard it was for me not to say yes."

He sighed. "I know. Guess I didn't see it from your point of view." Taking my arm, he pulled it over his stomach as we cuddled together.

More tears pooled behind my eyes. A part of me wanted to be selfish, and to say yes. I'd give anything to have him closer to me. But he had so much more to lose by leaving the team he loved, and the family and friends he had in North Carolina. Silence filled the air, except for the sound of the ocean, and Justin's heartbeat against my ear.

"Are we going to sleep out here?" I asked, voice thick with sadness.

He rolled over on top of me, and shook his head. "No. I'm going to make love to you. Right here, right now, for as long as you'll let me."

I ran my hands through his hair. "Hope you can last all night."

His lips pulled back, and they closed over mine. "Oh, I can, angel." He rubbed his growing arousal against my body. With one hand, he fumbled with my shorts, and slid them down my body along with my underwear. A deep growl rumbled in his chest when he felt how wet I was for him. "Hope you're ready for this."

Heart racing, I tore off my shirt, and tossed it on the sand. "More than ready."

He trailed a finger over my lips and down my chin to my breasts. "All right. You asked for this." Standing, he took off his shirt and shorts, making sure to slowly lower his boxers teasingly. He could put Magic Mike to shame with the way he moved his body.

His thick length hung heavy between his legs, and I had the overwhelming urge to taste him. My whole body trembled with need; I wanted all of him.

Keeping his gaze on mine, I could still see how heated they were, even if it was dark outside as he kissed his way up my body. He spread my legs and flicked his tongue over my clit, making me jerk. My body tingled, and I ached to feel more. His warm breath blew across it as he spoke, making the yearning worse. "You taste so fucking good," he groaned, his voice a low growl.

He licked me again, and I grabbed a handful of his hair and squeezed when he plunged his tongue inside. "Justin," I moaned.

I was so close to losing control, but he stopped and smirked up at me before licking a trail up to my breasts. "You are so evil." Two could play that game. I reached down between his legs and wrapped my hand around his arousal, stroking his length. He sucked in a breath and pushed himself up and down inside my hand. The tip of his cock grew wet, and I wiped it away with my thumb. Licking my lips, I brought it to my mouth and closed my eyes, moaning as I tasted him.

Groaning, he lowered his mouth to my breasts and sucked my nipple. "You'll be the death of me, angel." He grazed my skin with his teeth, and bit down gently at first, but then harder, a strangled cry escaping my lips. The pain of it felt amazing.

Reaching between my legs, he slipped a finger inside and groaned with how wet I was. "Do you have any idea how insanely hot that is? I love that I can make you this wet."

I bit my lip and grinned. "I kind of like it too."

He spread me wide and aligned himself at my opening. The moon glowed overhead, and I watched as another meteor streaked across the sky. I was never going to forget that moment for as long as I lived.

Slowly, Justin pushed, until he was as deep as he could go. I gasped and squeezed my legs tighter around his waist, pushing him deeper. We moved together as one, our bodies and souls fully connected. I'd never felt that level of intensity with anyone, not even my late husband.

My insides tightened, and I felt my release coming quick. Fisting his hands in my hair, Justin grunted with his thrusts, his cock pulsating inside me. I cried out as I finally reached the edge and trembled from the best orgasm of my life. Justin groaned and pounded his hips into mine as he chased his release, arms clutching me tight.

Leaning up on his elbows, Justin leaned down and kissed me, our bodies still connected. "I love you so fucking much it hurts."

I nodded. "Believe me, I know the feeling."

CHAPTER TWENTY-EIGHT

JUSTIN

THE TIME HAD COME TO say goodbye. I wasn't going to lie by saying it didn't hurt when Meghan said she didn't want me to move. Maybe it was stupid for even mentioning it, but dammit to hell, I wanted to be with her. I helped her parents load up their luggage in their rental car. James was already waiting for them at the airport with a private jet.

"Can I ride with you and Mommy?" Ellie asked, bouncing on her feet. "I've never been in a sports car before."

I picked her up in my arms, and she squeezed my neck. Meghan's parents watched us and smiled. "Of course, you can," I told her. "I wouldn't have it any other way."

Meghan came over and stole Ellie from me. "Come here, munchkin. Let's get you buckled up."

Meghan's parents walked over, and her mother hugged me. "Thanks, Justin. You've been a blessing to this family. I hope to see you soon."

I let her go. "You will."

Her father held out his hand. "Justin, it's been a pleasure. We need to go play golf one day when you got the time."

Grinning wide, I shook his hand. "Definitely. We might have a plus one when we do. I'm sure I can get Lucas to come out."

"That would be a dream come true."

Kimberly and Jackson said their goodbyes, and they all drove off to the airport. Ellie squealed as I started up the car. I was going to miss her little laugh, and her mother's smile. I contemplated not even taking them to the airport, and just keeping them with me until we got to Charlotte. That way, I'd have more time with them. Unfortunately, they had to get back. Meghan was supposed to be at her school the next day to set up her classroom.

The ride to the airport was silent, except for Ellie singing her favorite songs in the back. I held Meghan's hand, but she kept her face turned to the window. There were wet droplets on her shirt from her tears. It didn't take long to get to the small, private airport. Meghan's family was already there, talking to James, the pilot.

I parked beside them and grabbed Meghan's luggage out of my trunk. James came over and shook my hand before passing her luggage to one of his attendants. He led Meghan's family up the stairs, and they waved at me before disappearing inside.

There was no smile on Meghan's face, only tears. It broke my fucking heart. Never in my life had a woman ever made me feel like that. Ellie held onto Meghan's hand, and when she saw the tears on her mother's face, she started to cry as well.

"Oh no, peanut. You can't cry too. I don't think my heart can take it."

Ellie jumped in my arms, and sniffled. "I'm going to miss you. So is Mommy."

"I know," I whispered. "I'm going to miss you both too."

I set her down, and pulled Meghan into my arms. "I'll call you every day, okay?"

She nodded, her voice raspy and sad. "Okay. I didn't think it'd be so hard to say goodbye. We've been together every single day all summer long."

"I know, angel." I pressed my lips to hers, and breathed her in one last time. "I love you."

"I love you too. We'll see you soon."

Taking Ellie's hand, they walked up to the jet, and slowly climbed up the stairs. When they got to the door, they turned around and waved. I'd never felt so fucking miserable in my life.

THE SIX-AND-A-HALF-HOUR ride home started to drag. I'd only been on the road for two hours, and it felt like I'd driven for ages. I was hoping that once I got back on the ice it'd help me miss Meghan less. I needed something to keep my mind off of her. Now I knew what it felt like for Maddox when Lacey was living up in New York.

My phone rang, and Corey's name popped up on the radio screen. I pressed the button to accept his call. "Hey."

"Hey, yourself. You on the way home?"

I glanced around at the desolate, country road. "Yep. Should be back in about four hours."

"How did everything go? I haven't talked to you in a few days."

"Sorry. Been busy with Meghan's family."

The line went silent for a few seconds. I had no doubt he could tell something was wrong by my tone. "Anything you want to talk about?"

I laughed, but there was no humor in it. "If you only knew."

"Only knew what?"

Blowing out a heavy sigh, I ran a hand through my hair. "I offered to trade to another team to be close to Meghan."

"You what? That's insane."

I scoffed. "Tell me about it."

"You love her that much? Enough to change your whole life?"

"Wouldn't you do it for Hannah?" I snapped, hoping it backfired on him. He made it sound like I was crazy, when I knew for a fact he'd give up everything for Hannah.

"I would," he answered. "I guess it's just hard to imagine you being this in love with someone."

"Believe me, it's a new thing for me, but it feels so right. We're going to see each other as much as we can."

"Don't worry, brother. It'll all work out. If Maddox and Lacey could get through their issues, I have no doubt you and Meghan will."

I was going to make damn well sure we did. And I was going to make sure both Meghan and Ellie had everything they wanted. Speaking of Ellie … "So, I have a question."

"Yeah?"

Little Ellie's smiling face flashed through my mind. If she wanted to act, she was going to need help. "How would you feel about taking on a new client?"

"Seriously?" he snapped. "I'm not taking on anymore of your teammates. Dealing with you and Cliff is enough."

That made me laugh. "Thanks, asshole. I'm talking about Ellie. She wants to get into acting. I was thinking you could find her some commercial gigs to get her started."

Corey chuckled. "Damn, man. Never thought I'd see the day. Then again, you were always good with kids."

I kept replaying what Ellie said to me the night she had her nightmare. I honest to God hated that she never knew her dad, but I'd gotten so comfortable being that role for her the past couple of weeks. I was the only father figure she'd ever known, other than her grandfather and uncle. I wanted to be more.

"Will you do it?" I asked.

"Of course. I'll have to get used to the show business side of my job when you retire and go into movies, anyway."

"Actually, I have something else in mind for my future." Once I was done with hockey, I planned on getting away from the spotlight. It was going to be a new adventure for me.

CHAPTER TWENTY-NINE

MEGHAN

MY FAMILY WAS IMPRESSED WITH the private jet. The whole flight they talked about how amazing Justin was, and if I knew how much money he actually had. In all honesty, I didn't know anything about that. Justin and I never talked about his money, and I didn't want to. That wasn't the reason I was with him. Although it was nice having a plane all to ourselves.

"Thanks for bringing us home, sweetheart. It's nice to see this old thing running." She tapped the hood of Trey's truck and smiled. I hugged her, and then moved over to my dad to hug him. We'd left the truck at the airport so that when we got back, we wouldn't have to worry about someone taking us back to the ranch. Sadly, we never made it back together.

"Justin fixed it," I said, letting my dad go. I ran a hand gently down the old, blue paint. "It'll be Justin's truck when he comes in to visit."

My dad squeezed my arm. "Time moves fast. You'll see him again before you know it."

They waved at Ellie, and I got back in the truck. She buckled up quickly, and bounced in her seat. "Someone's excited about getting home," I said. I pulled out of my parents' driveway, and started on our way home. She was going to be in for a major surprise when she saw what all Justin and I had done.

Eyes twinkling, Ellie nodded excitedly. "I am," she squealed. "I'm ready to see the red barn."

Giggling, I reached over and ruffled her hair. "You're going to love it. It's a lot more awesome than the blah color we had before."

She danced around as if it was the best thing in the world. Even though I missed Justin, having Ellie around would cheer me up. She always had a way of making me smile. "What do you want to do when we get home?" I asked. "We have a little bit of time before we have to be at Sam and Emmett's for dinner."

Samantha wanted to catch up on everything, and I figured it was time to fill Emmett in about Justin. I prayed that he approved. His opinion wouldn't sway how I felt about Justin, but his approval would mean a lot. He was my only link to Trey, and I had to believe that he would want me to be happy, even if that meant finding love with someone else.

Grinning wide, Ellie shrugged. "I'm sure we'll figure it out when we get home."

"You are acting so strange right now," I said, studying her curiously.

A few minutes later, we turned into our driveway, and I slammed on the brakes. "Oh my God."

Ellie jumped up and down in her seat. "Come on, Mommy. Let's go."

Mouth gaping, I stared at our field, where not only did we

have our cows walking around, but there was also a familiar white and brown horse out there as well.

"It's Firefly, Mommy. I want to see him," she shouted, never once taking her eyes off of him. It broke her heart when I sold him. Hell, it broke mine as well. Firefly was who I talked to after Trey died. He was always there to listen to me during those late nights while Ellie slept.

I pulled further up into the driveway, and Danny Wilford was there, waiting by his truck. He was the principal at my school, and the man I'd sold Firefly to. As soon as I put the truck into park, Ellie jumped out and raced to the field.

Danny waved at me. "Hello there."

Confused, I got out and shut the truck door. I glanced back at Firefly, and then over to him. "What's going on?"

He nodded over at Firefly. "He's yours now. I got a nice offer from a young man who wanted to purchase him for you."

"Did this young man give you a name?" I asked, already knowing it was Justin. The man was too much. He'd done so much for me already.

Danny shook his head. "No, but I figured he was important to you."

A sad smile spread across my face. "He is. Thank you for bringing Firefly to me."

"You're welcome. I'm glad you were able to get Firefly back. I think he missed you."

Firefly walked beside Ellie over to the fence. He nudged me with his nose, and I rubbed him. "I've missed you too, boy. Welcome home."

Danny hopped in his truck and rolled the window down. "See you tomorrow at school, Meghan."

Ellie and I waved, and stood there with Firefly. Ellie climbed up on the fence so she could give Firefly a kiss. "Did you know about this?" I asked. "You seemed awfully excited to get home."

Snickering, she looked at me and nodded. "It was a secret. Justin made me promise."

"Sneaky." I pulled out my phone. He still had a couple hours before he'd even make it back to Charlotte.

"Well, hello," he answered.

Tears spilled down my cheeks. "Thank you, Justin. You have no idea how much Firefly means to me."

"You're welcome. I'm glad it makes you happy. I was waiting on you to call. Is Ellie close by?" he asked.

Brows furrowed, I looked over at Ellie. "Yeah."

"Can you put me on speakerphone, please?"

I did as he said, and tapped Ellie's shoulder. "Ellie-Bear, Justin wants to talk to you."

Her eyes lit up. "Hey, Justin."

"Hey, peanut. I have some good news for you and your mother. That is, if this is still what both of you want. Your mother has final say-so."

"What?" she squealed.

"Meghan, my brother wants to be her agent. We thought we'd start off small and get her into a few commercial auditions."

Ellie waved her hands in the air, and I had to steady her before she fell off the fence. "I think you stunned her," I said, laughing.

Tears filled Ellie's eyes. "Is this for real?"

"It is, peanut," Justin replied. "We can talk more about it when you two visit me next weekend."

Ellie jumped off the fence, flailing her body around into what I'd assume was her happy dance. Seeing her so ecstatic was just what I needed. I burst out laughing, and shook my head. "Justin, I wish you could see her dancing right now. She looks ridiculous."

"Are you okay with all of this?"

It scared me, but if Ellie wanted to do it, I wasn't going to hold her back. "Yeah, I'm fine. She's happy. That's all that matters."

UNTIL IT WAS TIME FOR dinner at Sam and Emmett's, I watched Ellie ride around on Firefly. In a way, I always knew I'd get him back one day. I'd kept our saddles in the barn for safe keeping until that time.

My leg shook the entire time we were in the truck, heading to Sam and Emmett's. Out of the corner of my eye, I could see Ellie staring at me. "Why are you so nervous?"

I tried to rub the tightness out of my chest, but nothing helped. "I need to tell Uncle Emmett about Justin. I don't know how he'll react."

Ellie shrugged as if it wasn't a big deal. "He'll like him. Who wouldn't?"

"It's not that simple, Ellie. Emmett's your father's brother. He's very protective of us. Not that you'd know, but Justin's had his fair share of mistakes. Uncle Emmett might not think he's good enough for us."

She waved me off. "Yeah, yeah, I know. There are plenty of times you thought I was asleep while you and Sam were watching his TV show. I know all about that horrible Miranda." Rolling her eyes, she shook her head in disgust. "Personally, I don't know what he saw in her. She's not nice."

Roaring in laughter, I leaned over and kissed her head.

"Trust me, your mother knows that from personal experience."

We pulled up to Sam and Emmett's house, and their door was open so we walked right on it. "We're here!" I shouted.

Samantha burst into the room, and held her arms out for Ellie. "There's my sweet girl!"

Ellie hugged her and giggled. "We have so much to tell you."

Samantha's brows lifted as she looked at me. "I bet. I have a lot to tell your mother as well. Why don't you go outside and say hey to Uncle Emmett? He's at the grill." Ellie took off, and Samantha stared at me, biting her lip sheepishly.

"Uh-oh, what's wrong?" I asked.

She closed her eyes. "Emmett knows about you and Justin already."

That was not what I wanted to hear. "What? How?"

The back door slammed shut, and he appeared with Ellie in his arms. "Through a guy at work. His wife saw you in the tabloids, and he showed it to me. I had no clue what to say. And when I asked Samantha about it, she told me you were seeing him."

Ellie squeezed him around the neck. "He's so sweet, Uncle Emmett. We got to ride in his private jet, we had the whole ice cream store to ourselves, and he taught me how to boogie board."

Emmett's eyes widened, and he smiled. "Wow. Looks like you know him pretty well then."

Ellie nodded. "I do. We're going to visit him next weekend."

Emmett set her down, and nodded toward the kitchen. "Why don't you go sneak one of Aunt Sam's famous chocolate chip cookies? They're hot out of the oven. Only one though. We don't want you ruining your dinner."

She hurried off, and he turned to me, crossing his arms

over his chest. "Why didn't you tell me? He was over there that day I stopped by, wasn't he?"

I nodded. "It's a long story. He didn't want anyone knowing he was in Wyoming, and I wasn't ready for anyone to see him with me."

"And you are now?" he asked.

"Yes. I love him."

Swooning, Samantha placed a hand over her heart. "It's about time."

Emmett shook his head, regarding me curiously. "Are you sure this is what you want, Meg? The life of a celebrity is never private. You can't go anywhere without someone snapping pictures of you."

"I know. It's a sacrifice I'm willing to make."

"And Ellie? What about her?"

Samantha and I both looked at each other and laughed. "Ellie will be fine," Samantha said, "She'll be the one posing for the pictures. That girl loves the spotlight."

Emmett cracked a smile. "Yeah, you're right. She does."

"He's a good guy, Emmett, and he's wonderful with Ellie. She loves him too."

His eyes saddened, and his gaze landed on a picture of him and Trey. "Trey would want you to be happy. And Justin can give you and Ellie the things he never got the chance to give."

Tears sprung to my eyes. "Does that mean you're not mad?"

He closed the distance, and hugged me. "Not at all. Still a little shocked, but I'm happy for you. But if he hurts you and Ellie, I'll kick his ass."

Giggling, I let him go. "If he does, I'll kick his ass myself."

Samantha pushed between us, and put her arms around us. "Now that it's settled, and Meghan's dating a famous superstar, it's time to eat. I'm starving." We walked into the kitchen just in time to catch Ellie stealing a second cookie. She shoved it in her mouth, and we all laughed.

"So when do I get to meet this famous boyfriend?" Emmett asked.

"Soon."

CHAPTER THIRTY

JUSTIN

Being on the ice felt fucking amazing. It was like I'd never been away from it. I skated better than I'd ever skated before. Usually, Maddox would be my wingman, but since he retired, Cliff had taken his spot.

I patted his shoulder as we exited the ice. "You did pretty good today."

Cliff beamed. "Thanks. We make a good team."

"All right, all right, get out of my way, pansies," Dallas said from behind. "I got to get home to my wife."

Cliff and I moved out of his way, and Dallas winked. "I knew I could get you out of my way."

I slapped him over the head. "You're such an ass."

I tore off my gear as soon as we got into the locker room. My phone beeped inside my locker, and I hurried to get it out. It was from a couple hours ago, but it was a picture of

Meghan in her classroom, posing for the camera, along with the text *I miss you*.

The smile she gave me wasn't her happy one; it was sad. I'd learned to know the difference between them from spending so much time with her. Cliff and Dallas were right across from me, so I held up my phone and got in the picture.

"Smile, cocksuckers."

They smiled for the camera, and I sent it to her.

Me: I miss you too!

Cliff chuckled. "Who was that to?"

Dallas put his arm around his shoulders. "His girlfriend. While you were busy this summer, our boy here fell in love."

Cliff threw his jersey at me. "What the hell, man? You didn't tell me this shit. Now I know why you never returned any of my calls."

I tossed his jersey back at him, hitting him right in the face. "I was busy. Not that it's any of your damn business," I said, laughing.

"How is it going, anyway?" Dallas asked. "You doing okay with the distance?"

Sitting down on the bench, I took off my skates. How was I doing? Not too damn good now that I had time to think about it. Being on the ice helped, but I couldn't be out there twenty-four-seven. "I'm fine. She and Ellie are visiting next weekend."

Cliff sat down across from me. "Who's Ellie?"

"Her daughter," I said, gauging his reaction.

His eyes widened in shock. "Wow. Didn't see that coming. Are you getting all domesticated on us now?"

Dallas smacked him on the head. "What the fuck, man? There is nothing wrong with that. I'm domesticated, so what?"

Cliff held his hands up in defeat. "Okay, wrong choice of words. I take it back." When Dallas turned away, he rubbed his head. "I'll just have to find someone else to party with."

"True," I said. "I'm done." It didn't bother me at all. I didn't care about going out to parties and drinking all night. At least, not without Meghan. Even then, it didn't interest me to be wild and crazy like I used to be.

"I guess that means you're not hanging out at the bar with me and some of the guys tonight?" Cliff asked.

I shook my head. "Can't. I told Meghan and Ellie I'd video chat with them at seven."

Cliff stared at me without a single blink. "Okay, what have you done with the real Justin Davis?"

It was a good question. I didn't know who I really was until I went to Wyoming and met Meghan. For the first time in my life, I was allowed to be myself. No cameras. No paparazzi following me around. It was the best time I'd ever had.

With a smile on my face, I stared right back at Cliff. "This is the real me."

Dallas' phone rang, and when he answered, he almost fell over the bench. He tossed his gear into his locker, and quickly threw on his clothes. As soon as he hung up the phone, he jumped up on the bench and shouted, "I'm going to be a father tonight, cocksuckers!"

The locker room erupted in cheers. "Was that her on the phone?" I asked, trying my best to hurry and get dressed.

Dallas slung his bag over his shoulder. "Yep. Her water broke. I have to hurry home and get her to the hospital."

That was the best news I'd heard all day. If only Callie could see how excited he was. Dallas took off for the door, and I shouted after him. "I'll meet you at the hospital!"

Cliff shook his head and smiled. "Maybe I need to find a woman and settle down. Your situation is a little different from Dallas's, but by the way you mentioned Ellie's name, you seem to be happy with the thought of being a father."

"I am," I admitted honestly. "It's a good feeling." I packed up my stuff and headed for the door. I had a niece to meet.

By the time I made it to the hospital, Callie was already in a birthing room, prepping for the delivery. Dallas was telling everyone who would listen that the labor was going so fast because his daughter was so excited to meet him.

It was closing in on seven o'clock, and right on time, my phone rang with a video call. Thankfully, there was no one in the waiting room. Meghan waved at me with Ellie on her lap.

"Hey, babe," she said.

"Hey, pretty ladies. Did you have a good day?"

Ellie nodded excitedly. "I helped Mommy while she decorated her classroom, and then we came home and rode Firefly."

"That sounds like fun. I miss you guys."

Meghan held Ellie closer. "We miss you too." Her gaze narrowed. "Where are you? Looks like the hospital."

"It is," I answered.

Ellie gasped. "Oh no. Are you sick?"

I burst out laughing. "No, peanut. My sister's having her baby. I wanted to be here."

"Is it a girl or boy?" she asked, clapping her hands excitedly.

"Girl. I don't know her name yet, but I'll let you know when I find out."

Dallas came into the waiting room, and saw them on the video. He sat beside me and waved at them.

Meghan's eyes widened and she smiled. "Hey, Dallas. Congratulations. I hate I can't be there. I'd love to see your little girl."

He placed a hand over his heart. "Thank you. She's so beautiful."

"What did you name her?" Ellie asked.

Dallas chuckled, and moved closer to the camera. "You must be Ellie. It's so nice to finally meet you. Justin's told us a lot about you. Callie and I named her Rowan."

"That's a very pretty name," Meghan said. Ellie agreed with a nod.

Dallas waved at them one last time. "Thank you again. You'll be able to see her when you guys visit next weekend." He squeezed my shoulder. "I'm going back to the room. When you get done here, come to the room."

Once he was gone, I looked at my girls and sighed. "Next weekend seems so far away."

Meghan nodded, but there was a hint of tears in her eyes. "It does, but at least we can see each other this way."

It wasn't good enough, but it was all we had. "I love you," I said. "Both of you."

Ellie blew me a kiss. "We love you too."

Meghan gave me a sad smile, and blew me a kiss as well. "I love you. Give your little niece a snuggle for me."

"I will." The call ended, and I went straight to Callie's room. She was in the bed, tears in her eyes as she watched Dallas holding their baby. I lightly tapped the door, and caught her attention. "Knock, knock."

Her eyes lit up, and she waved me in. "Hey. Come see your niece."

Dallas stood and nodded for me to take a seat on the couch. When I did, he gently placed the baby in my arms. She was so tiny, all bundled up in a snug pink blanket. There was even a small patch of blonde hair on her head.

"Sorry, Dallas, but your daughter has blonde hair like me and her mother. She's definitely going to take after the Davis side of the family."

Dallas walked over to the bed and kissed Callie on the lips. "That's perfectly fine with me. I'll just have my shotgun ready when she starts to date."

Callie laid her head back on the bed and turned to me. "Oh, dear Lord, I pray for my daughter. She's going to have a hard time when she becomes a teenager."

I shrugged. "Hey, it's a father's job to torment the boyfriends."

Dallas rubbed a hand soothingly over her head. "Want anything? I figured you'd be dying for a blueberry bagel with cream cheese right about now."

"Yes," she breathed. "That'd be great."

Dallas looked over at me. "Do you mind staying here with her while I run out for a second?"

Rowan squirmed a little in my arms, and I smiled down at her. "Not at all." Once he was gone, all I did was hold Rowan and stare at her. It made me realize how much I really wanted a family of my own.

"How's Meghan?" Callie asked.

"Good," I said, meeting her tired gaze. "Dallas got to meet Ellie out in the waiting room when I was video chatting with them. They can't wait to visit next weekend and see you all."

Callie smiled. "Can't wait to see them, and meet little Ellie." I don't know what passed across my face, but Callie could tell something was wrong. "What's on your mind, Justin? Is it Meghan?"

It was hard to hide my true feelings. "Yes," I answered truthfully. "I offered to find a way to get traded to Colorado to be closer to her."

She gasped. "Wow. What'd she say?"

I shook my head. "She said no. That I'd regret my decision, and resent her."

"Would you?" Callie asked.

"No." I didn't even have to think about the answer. I knew what I wanted, and what I was sacrificing. She was worth it all.

Callie shrugged. "Then go after what you want. I can see it on your face that you're miserable without her. It's not easy when you love someone so much and you can't be with them."

With a heavy sigh, I stood, still cradling little Rowan in my arms. "What if I get out there and tell her all of this, and she's still afraid of me making the move?"

Callie looked right into my eyes. "Then make her see that it's the right decision. You won't be happy until you do."

Carefully, I handed Rowan back to her. "You're right. I won't. I know what I have to do."

CHAPTER THIRTY-ONE

MEGHAN

"Ellie-Bear, do you want a bowl of cereal before we go?" I called out.

"Yes, please." Her voice echoed from the bathroom.

I pulled out her Frosted Flakes from the cabinet, and poured some in a bowl. The summer was coming to an end, which meant she had to get used to getting up early again for school. It was going to be strange getting back into a normal routine after the summer I had. So many things had changed. A part of me kept thinking I'd see Justin walking up my driveway, dressed in his jeans and cowboy hat. He'd worked hard on my fence and barn. Every time I looked at them, memories would flash in my mind. It only made me realize how much I missed him.

"Mommy?"

Jerking away from the window, I grabbed my chest. Ellie stood there, still dressed in her pink and yellow nightgown.

"You scared me," I gasped. "I thought you'd be dressed by now. We're leaving for the school in forty-five minutes. I still have some decorating to do."

She nodded. "I know. I have my clothes picked out already."

I kissed her head, and nudged her toward the kitchen table. "Perfect. Let me get the milk, and you can eat." I poured the milk into her bowl, and sat down across from her. She spooned some into her mouth, her lips turned down in a frown. "Honey, you okay?"

She shrugged. "Just thinking."

"About what?"

Her head lifted, and she met my gaze. "You."

"What about me?"

She shrugged again. "I don't know. You seem so sad all the time. I know you miss Justin."

My chest ached, and it took all I had not to try and rub the pain away. Nothing helped. "I do, Ellie. I miss him a lot."

"Then why did you tell him not to move?"

I shook my head. "It's not that simple, sweetheart. I don't want him switching teams just to be near us. It's not fair to him."

She spooned a bite of cereal into her mouth, staring at me as if she was the wise one in the family. "We could move to North Carolina."

That caught me off guard. "What?"

"We could move to North Carolina," she repeated, the sound of her cereal crunching between her teeth. "That way, Justin doesn't have to leave his team."

"But what about us? You'd be leaving your friends, and I'd be leaving my job. Not to mention, Maw Maw and Paw Paw are here."

She slid her bowl to the side and came over to sit on my

lap. "I can make friends anywhere, Mommy. And you're a teacher, so you can get a job at any school."

It was true, but …

"What about Maw Maw and Paw Paw, and Aunt Kimberly?" I asked.

She shrugged. "They can visit. Maw Maw and Paw Paw are planning to move to the beach house anyway. They'll already be in North Carolina."

Who knew that my eight-year-old would have so much wisdom at such a young age. But could it be possible? Was it really that easy?

I shook my head. "We can't, Ellie. I can't go to Justin and tell him we'll move out there. What if he's not ready for that?"

Her little hands clutched my face. "He loves us, Mommy. If he was ready to move out here to be with us, why would he not want us there to be with him? I think it'll be fun."

"What if he tells me no, just like I told him?"

She slid her arms around my neck, and laid her head on my shoulder. "What is it you always tell me when I *think* something's too hard to do?"

Holding her tight, I breathed her in and smiled. "You never know until try." Tears sprung to my eyes. "How did you get to be so smart?"

She let me go, and smiled. "I take after my mother."

"All right, let's do this. I'll drop you off at Maw Maw and Paw Paw's, and then I'll head to the airport."

Squealing, she jumped off my lap. "I'll be dressed and ready to go in two minutes."

Heart racing, I hurried to my bedroom and packed a bag. It was rash, and completely sudden, but it felt right. Ellie was right … I had to try.

It turned out there was a flight leaving for Charlotte in just three hours. I had plenty of time to get Ellie to my parents and get to the airport.

"Are you nervous?" Ellie asked.

My hands shook, but I gripped the steering wheel so hard so she couldn't tell. "No, not at all."

She giggled. "I'm glad you don't want to be an actress. Justin's going to be happy to see you."

"I hope so, honey. It'll definitely be a surprise."

We pulled down my parents' driveway, and they were outside waiting on us. I rolled down my window, and as soon as the truck came to a stop, Ellie hugged my neck and hopped out. "Have fun, Mommy. I love you."

"I love you too."

Ellie latched onto my father's leg, and he picked her up. They waved one more time before disappearing inside the house. My mother came over to my side of the truck, grinning as if she knew something I didn't.

"You think I'm stupid for going, don't you?"

She shook her head. "On the contrary," she replied, leaning her arms on my window, "I'm surprised it took you this long to decide to go. I thought you would've agreed to this before Justin left town."

"Really?" That shocked me.

"Oh yeah. I knew the long-distance thing wasn't going to last. You made it two days."

Groaning, I leaned my head against the wheel. "I tried,

Mom. I miss him so much. What scares me is uprooting Ellie. I don't want her life having to change because of me."

She tapped my shoulder. "Her life *is* going to change, and so is yours, no matter what you do. Stay here, move there, it doesn't matter. What matters is that you follow your heart. Ellie will be loved no matter where you go, so don't worry about her." Sighing, I leaned back and met her gaze. "Besides," she said, patting my cheek, "your father and I are moving to the beach house in the spring. We'll just be six hours away from you. You don't have to worry about us."

That was a huge relief, because they were one of the reasons why I didn't want to leave Wyoming. It was like a heavy weight had been lifted. "Thanks, Mom. I think I needed to hear that."

She winked. "Go get your man."

"I will."

There was still plenty of time to get to the airport. When I arrived, there was still almost two hours until takeoff. I grabbed my bag and my purse, and walked inside the airport to the airline ticket counter.

The woman smiled at me as I put my luggage on the scale. "Name, please," she said. "And I need to see your license so I can get you checked in."

"Sure thing." I unzipped my purse, and reached in, only to find that I didn't have my wallet. Panic consumed me, and I frantically checked the floor. Then I realized I'd left my wallet on the kitchen counter after I hastily ordered the plane ticket. I'd forgotten to put it back in my purse.

"Is everything okay?" the woman asked.

"No," I groaned, slapping a hand to my forehead. "I left my wallet at home." It was thirty minutes home, and then another thirty back. Luckily, I still had two hours left. I grabbed my luggage off the scale. "I have to run home and get it. I'll be back."

She nodded. "Okay." I could see the sympathy on her face. I prayed like hell there wasn't a traffic jam or a herd of moose trying to cross the road on my way home. Carrying my luggage, I ran as fast as I could out of the airport. It was times like this I wished I hadn't driven the old truck. I needed my Toyota 4Runner to haul ass down the highway.

Thankfully, I made it home without any problems. I rushed inside the house, my heart thumping so hard it made my chest hurt. My wallet was on the counter exactly where I left it. I grabbed it up, and ran out the door, my fingers shaking as I tried to lock it.

When I turned around, it felt like I ran into a brick wall. My wallet fell to the ground, and I almost did as well, but a set of muscled arms held me in place. I looked up, and there he was.

"What the hell?" I gasped.

Chuckling, Justin pulled me into his arms. "That's the kind of greeting I get? Reminds me of the first time we met."

I was in shock. "No, that's not what I meant. I'm just surprised. What are you doing here?"

His lips pulled back slyly. "I'm here for you. I decided I'm not taking no for an answer."

A flood of emotions swirled through me. I couldn't even think straight. "What do you mean?"

"I mean," he said, holding me tighter, "is that I can't stand being anywhere without you. I'm going to ask to be traded." A burst of laughter roared out of my chest, and he stared at me as if I'd slapped him on the face. That wasn't my intent. If he only knew my plan. Brows furrowed, he stepped back. "Why are you laughing?"

"Because!" I cried, grabbing his hands to pull him closer, "If you must know, I was on my way back to the airport."

"For what?"

"To be with you."

He shook his head. "I don't understand."

I brought one of his hands up to my face, loving the feel of him against my cheek. "I don't want you changing teams, Justin. And I don't want you moving out this way."

His gaze saddened. "What do you want then?"

Lifting up on my toes, I kissed him. "You. That's why I'm moving to Charlotte. I was getting on a plane so I could tell you face to face. Seeing you here, and your willingness to change your life for me and Ellie, only makes my decision that much easier." I kissed him again. "Please say you'll let me do this."

At first, he seemed open to it, but then he shook his head. "What about your parents and Ellie? I don't want you leaving your family."

I placed a finger over his lips. "Ellie is more than excited about the change, and my parents are moving to Nags Head. It's all working out."

"Are you sure?"

He closed the distance, and I melted against him. "More than sure. I want to be where you are."

"You have no idea how amazing it feels to hear you say that."

Crushing me to his chest, I didn't care if I could barely breathe. It felt good knowing he was there. "Don't you have hockey practice tomorrow?"

He kissed the side of my neck. "I do. James is at the airport, waiting to take me back on the jet." Slowly, he pulled away, his gaze landing on my lips. "But I have a couple hours to spare. I figured we could go find Ellie and tell her the good news."

I bit my lip. "We can do that, but there's one thing I want to do first."

"Oh yeah? What's that?"

Fisting his shirt in my grasp, I pulled him down to me. "I think you know."

"Let's not waste any time then." He wrapped his arms around my waist and lifted me up, kissing his way down my neck to the tops of my breasts.

With my legs around his waist, he carried me inside and slammed the door, ripping my shirt off before we could even get to the bedroom. Giggling, I looked down at the tattered garment on the ground and then up to him. His gaze was raw.

"I'll get you another one," he assured me.

Leaning me against the wall, Justin lifted my bra and cupped my breast in his hand, shifting me up so he could suck my nipple between his teeth. Closing my eyes, I moaned and held him close, my insides tightening. I could feel the blood rushing to the spot between my legs that ached to feel Justin's touch. Only one gentle stroke and I would be completely lost and at his mercy.

"Justin," I breathed, arching my back.

Chuckling, he reached around behind my back and unclasped my bra, letting it fall to the floor. He stood back and looked up and down my body as I straddled him, his cock getting harder between my legs.

"You are so beautiful, Meghan," he murmured, sliding a strand of my hair off my forehead. "I promise I'll give you everything you want."

"I'll have everything I want if I have you," I answered him softly.

Slowly, he leaned forward and placed his forehead to mine, breathing me in. "And you do. You have all of me."

"And you have all of me."

He was a dangerous man on the ice, yet so gentle in his touches. My God, I was so in love with him. I shouldn't have let it happen, but I couldn't fight it. I didn't regret it one bit. He was the best worst decision I could've ever made for myself.

He carried me down the hall to my bedroom. Plucking at his shirt, I demanded, "This needs to come off."

He smirked and lifted one arm. I promptly tugged his shirt over his head, and he let it fall to the floor. I ran my hands over his arms and down his washboard abs as he gently laid me down on my king-sized bed.

Starting at my lips, he trailed his finger down my neck, in between my breasts, and on to my shorts, which he slid down my legs and tossed to the side. His hands were warm as he ran them up my legs to spread them, caressing my thighs.

Smirking, he lowered his shorts to the floor and slowly climbed onto the bed. Biting my lip, I spread my legs as he slowly crawled up my body. He rested off to the side, his thick length pressing into my thigh as he turned me to him.

"Most people don't know the real me, Meghan. But with you … I've never been afraid to show you."

"I'm glad," I murmured wholeheartedly. "I love the real you."

Spreading my legs with his knee, he smiled down at me and covered my body with his, leaning on his elbows to keep his full weight off of me. I was utterly at his mercy, and I loved it.

"You've made me so happy, angel," he claimed, brushing his fingers down my cheek.

"I have?" I asked, kissing his fingers as be brushed them over my lips.

He nodded. "I know you love it here in Wyoming, and leaving it is giving up a part of yourself."

"I'd do anything for you, Justin."

He lowered his lips to mine and I closed my eyes, loving the way my lips tingled every time they touched his. "And I'd do anything for you," he answered. "That's why I'll make sure we spend every bit of free time and the summer doing exactly what you want. If you want to spend it here, we can. If you want to spend it with your family, we can do that too. I want you to know that I'm at your mercy. Whatever you say goes."

Looking at him, I smiled and wrapped my legs around his waist, feeling his cock jump in anticipation as I rubbed against it. "I like the sound of that. You might regret saying it."

He bit his lip. "Not at all."

"Then make love to me, Justin. That's what I want you to do."

Ever so gently, Justin unhooked my legs and slid his hand up the inside of my thigh, opening my legs further. Lowering his head, he flicked his tongue across my clit. I gasped.

When he chuckled, his breath fanned across my body, making it even more sensitive. His tongue worked wonders. Every time he pushed it inside of me, he rolled it around, tasting me while nuzzling my clit with his nose, keeping me stimulated.

"Justin," I moaned, fisting my hands in his hair. I was so close.

"That's right, angel. Let me make you come."

I screamed out his name as the force of my release had me arching off the bed, my hands still tangled in his hair. Slowly, I released my hands and brought them to my chest, where my heart thumped wildly.

"I think you're ready now," he claimed, licking his lips.

I lowered my hand and wrapped it around him. As I glided my hand up and down his cock, Justin pushed his length through my hand, biting his lip as he watched me. I loved seeing that wild, primal look in his eyes.

"Mmm … that feels so good, angel."

The more I rubbed him, the more he trembled, twisting in my grip.

"That's enough, Meghan. I'm a little too worked up to be played with."

"Next time, then," I teased.

He lowered himself onto my body and bit my lip, tugging on it. "I look forward to it."

He rocked his hips against mine, and his arousal moved between my legs, rubbing along the slit, getting nice and wet. Then the tip found its mark, pushing inside, stretching me. Taking a deep breath, I closed my eyes and felt a tender kiss before he slowly pressed in the rest of the way. The pain of it made my eyes water, but it was a good pain. In fact, I needed more.

Capturing his face in my hands, I bit his lip and sucked on it as hard as I could. "Harder. I promise I won't break."

He growled low and gripped the edges of the pillow beneath my head. "Fuck, you're killing me. I don't want to hurt you."

I was ready to feel the heat, the intensity. Most of our love-making had been passionate and gentle, but I wanted it hard and raw. "You won't. Now stop holding back."

Almost immediately, his breathing picked up and his eyes darkened, the intensity building in the room. I shivered in response and gripped my legs tighter around his waist, rocking my hips hard against his. That was his undoing.

Fisting his hands in my hair, he pulled my head to the side and bit down on my neck, his thrusts growing deeper and faster. I screamed out in pleasure, but Justin silenced me by closing his lips over mine. The harder he pushed his body into me, the closer I was to losing control. I could tell he was close. As soon as I started to clench down on him, he released my hair and brought his hands down to my face, keeping his eyes locked on mine.

Digging my nails into his skin, I rode wave after wave of pure bliss as the longest damn orgasm of my life rocked through my body. It only intensified when Justin growled in my ear, biting down on my lobe as he too released, pulsating inside of me.

Breathing hard, he lifted up on his elbows and smiled down at me.

I smiled back. The morning was everything I could've wanted and more.

"Are you okay?" he asked.

I was more than okay. However, looking down at his lips, he definitely wasn't. His bottom lip was red and swollen. I pointed at it and chuckled. "I'm perfectly fine, but I can't say the same about you."

"What are you talking about?"

Biting my lip, I looked down at his and cringed. "I kind of left a mark on your lip. It's going to be embarrassing when we go to my parents' house to get Ellie."

He didn't seem to care by the grin on his face. "Is it bad? We can tell Ellie you accidentally punched me when I startled you."

The thought made me laugh. "That could very well work. Unfortunately, my parents will know the truth."

With a smirk, he tilted my head to the side. "It's not like they don't know already. You, however, need a good story for your neck."

I waved him off. "That's what makeup is for." We both laughed, and I placed a hand over his chest, loving the way it felt. "Think you can handle living with two girls? It's a lot to ask of you."

He shook his head. "No, it's not. It's what I want. And speaking of which, I need to get one of my spare bedrooms ready for Ellie."

"Go with unicorns. That's what she's into right now."

His smile broadened. "I can do that. You about ready to tell her the good news?"

I was more than excited. I kissed him quick, and jumped out of bed. "Yep. Let's go."

CHAPTER
THIRTY-TWO

MEGHAN

"Are you excited?" Justin asked.

Ellie squealed. "Yes!"

She gawked out the window at all the huge houses we passed by. Justin had flown in the private jet to pick us up from Wyoming so he could see my family one last time before we left for good. It'd been two weeks since we'd seen him, but that was only because he had been busy getting his house ready for us. Ellie was going to be in for a treat.

We'd left all of our furniture in Wyoming, but one day, we'd be back there for good. Until then, we were going to visit as much as we could. Kimberly and Jackson were going to take care of Firefly in the meantime. My nieces loved him. I wanted to bring him to North Carolina, but he belonged in the Wyoming mountains. He'd be happier there.

In just two days, Ellie would be starting a new school. I was terrified, but she was excited about it. I'd already talked to her teacher, and they were ecstatic to have her. Since I wasn't in town during orientation, Justin had gone to drop off her school supplies and say hello. Needless to say, it caused quite a few heads to turn, but Ellie's teacher promised me that everything would run smoothly. It turns out they were going to have a position available after Christmas. I looked forward to getting back to teaching, but it was going to be nice to have a few months to get used to the move.

We pulled up at Justin's house, and he pressed the button to open the gate. Ellie's mouth dropped as she looked up at the huge mansion. "This is your house?" she asked, her voice just above a whisper.

Justin tapped her chin. "It's yours now too. Come on."

We got out, and she grabbed my hand, still looking stunned. I pulled her inside, and she went straight to the back door. "You have a pool? It's ginormous!"

Justin chuckled. "And it's heated. We can swim in the winter." We followed her into the kitchen, where she grabbed a grape out of the fruit bowl. Justin nudged her toward the refrigerator. "Why don't you look in the freezer?"

Ellie ran over and opened it up. Inside was every single Ben and Jerry's flavor you could imagine. "Oh my goodness. This is heaven."

Justin and I burst out laughing. "I told you she'd say that," I said. He'd asked to know every little thing that Ellie liked. He wanted to make sure she had everything she'd ever need. I didn't want her to turn into a spoiled brat, but she deserved way more than I could ever give her. Although I had a feeling I was going to have to monitor what all Justin gave her. It was clear he was smitten by her.

Justin bent down and Ellie climbed on his back. "Ready to see your room?"

She squealed, and held on. "Yes."

He carried her upstairs, and I giggled the whole way. The

door to her room was shut, and even I had no clue what it looked like. Justin assured me Ellie would love it. When he opened the door, it was a magical paradise. He let her down, and she stared at everything in awe. The walls were a light lilac, and the bedspread had a giant unicorn on it, with soft pastel colors. It was all glitter and sunshine.

Gasping, she ran inside and picked up the giant white stuffed unicorn in the corner. It was like watching her at Christmas time. "Thank you! Thank you! This is so pretty."

Justin leaned against the doorframe. "Think you'll like living here?" he asked her.

She nodded, and searched around the room. "Oh, yeah. Does this mean you two are going to get married?"

Silence filled the room, but Justin looked at me with a devilish grin. I could see myself marrying him, but we hadn't talked about it yet. The thought of it excited me. I wanted to see what it was like being in the spotlight with him before we made any of those kinds of decisions. Ellie stared at us, waiting.

Justin shrugged. "I don't know if your mommy wants to marry me. She hasn't said a word about it."

Ellie turned her gaze to me. "Do you, Mommy?"

I glared at him, and then looked over at Ellie, smiling. "Maybe," I replied. "Right now, we're going to stay here for a while and see how it goes. How does that sound?"

She shrugged. "Okay."

Justin chuckled, and nodded downstairs. "The biggest surprise is downstairs, peanut. Ready to see what it is?"

Jumping up and down, she clapped her hands excitedly. We all went downstairs to the basement, where the movie theater was. It just so happened that Justin had *Ice Princess* already playing on the screen. Ellie flopped down in one of the recliners, mesmerized by it all. Justin pulled me out into the hallway, still giving me that mischievous grin.

I smacked his arm. "Thanks for putting me on the spot."

He winked. "I was curious to see what you'd say."

"Did you not like my answer?"

He shrugged. "Hard to tell. You said maybe, which gives me hope, but other than that, I didn't get much from it."

"Maybe you'll just have to ask me and find out."

Pulling me close, he kissed me, nipping by bottom lip. "I might just do that one day."

EPILOGUE

MEGHAN

CLOSING MY EYES, I BREATHED in the sea air as it whipped all around me. The sound of the waves was music to my ears. It wasn't as hot in October at the Outer Banks as it was this summer, of course, but it was still warm. The sand was cool under my feet, and for the first time in months, I had a book in my hands. It was nice to sit back and relax with my favorite two people, who were making a sand castle beside me. Nothing could be more perfect. It was nice having a private jet whenever we wanted. With Justin having a couple days off, we were able to fly to the beach house.

Ever since Ellie and I were discovered at Justin's first hockey game, it'd been a whirlwind of craziness. We'd done numerous interviews, and were even on a talk show. It was actually quite exciting. Justin had warned me that it was just the beginning. Ellie was ecstatic about it all. She'd already landed two commercial gigs, and filming was set to begin in a few weeks.

Ellie giggled, and I turned my attention away from the crashing waves. "What are you laughing at, Ellie-Bear?" I asked. She was so cute in her black and pink bathing suit and her floppy hat. And as always, Justin was sexy as hell with his chiseled abs, wearing a pair of navy swim trunks.

Ellie and Justin crouched down next to the sand castle, whispering to each other. She lifted her head and waved. "Nothing. We're just talking about hockey. I can't wait for the game next week. They're so fun."

Justin winked. "She likes to watch me score."

"Don't we all," I teased, winking back. "Your team played amazing last week. I sense another Stanley Cup win next year."

Ellie squealed. "That would be awesome." She wrapped her arms Justin's neck and batted her eyelashes at him. "I know something else that would be awesome."

Chuckling, he stood, and she latched on to him. "What is it peanut?"

"Well … I was hoping you'd let me invite Ashlynn over next Saturday for a playdate." Ashlynn was her best friend at school. I was happy she was able to make friends so quickly. In another couple of months, I was going to be a teacher at her school.

Justin shook his head, and smiled over at me. "You see this? She thinks that by giving me her puppy-dog eyes that I'm going to say yes to everything she asks."

I tried to hide my smile and failed. "She has that effect on people."

Justin kissed her forehead, and set her down. "Fine. She can come over as long as it's okay with her parents."

"I'll talk to her mother," I said. "We've been texting back

and forth the past couple of weeks. I promised her we'd get coffee when I got back into town."

His smile broadened. "I'm happy to see you making friends. You can always invite Grant, Samantha and Emmett, and whoever you want to stay with us one weekend. I know you miss everyone from Wyoming."

"I might just do that." He'd told me for weeks that I could, but I'd been so busy getting settled in that it was hard to imagine having guests. I did miss my family and friends.

Ellie pulled on Justin's arm, and he knelt down. She whispered something in his ear, and he nodded.

"What's with all the secrets?" I asked, narrowing my gaze at them. "Is there something going on I should know about?"

Justin looked up at me, and smiled. "Actually, there is. Ellie wants you to look at our sand castle."

Ellie reached for my hands, and I stood. Their sand castle had a moat that went all the way around it, and it stood about three feet tall. They'd worked on it for about four hours. I stood in front of it, and nodded in approval. "It's magnificent. I love it."

Justin nudged me closer. "Why don't you take a look inside?"

Carefully, I stepped over the moat and peeked inside the castle doorway. There was something inside, but I couldn't tell what it was. "What is it?" I asked.

Ellie snickered, which made Justin laugh. "Reach in there and find out."

Turning around, I glared at them. "So help me God, if you put a crab in there or something gross like seaweed, I'm going to beat you both."

Ellie groaned impatiently. "Just do it, Mommy."

Clenching my teeth together, I reached inside, not being able to see a damn thing. I was terrified of touching something slimy. When my fingers tapped something hard, I breathed a sigh of relief. It wasn't anything alive. I grabbed the object and slowly pulled it out. It wasn't until I got a good look at it that I realized what it was.

The breath whooshed out of my lungs. Resting in my hands was a small, black box. Justin took my elbow, and helped me over the moat while Ellie bounced on her feet excitedly. Clearing his throat, he grabbed the box and knelt down on one knee. I looked around—no one was on the beach. It was just us.

"Meghan," he murmured, opening the box. The diamond ring glittered in the sun.

I slapped a hand over my mouth. "Oh my God."

Justin pulled out the ring, and gently took my hand, his emerald eyes staring up into mine. "I love you, Meghan. By now, you know that I'd do anything for you and Ellie. I'd given a lot of thought of how I was going to do this. Yes, I could've taken you to the island, or anywhere around the world, but this place is special for us. It's where I first met Ellie, and where our relationship turned into something more." I looked over at Ellie, her eyes glistening and lip quivering. Justin pulled her close, and hugged her. "I made sure to ask this little one's permission first. We had a heart to heart."

"Seriously? You knew about this?" I asked her.

She nodded. "Justin made me promise not to tell." The girl was good at keeping her word. She looked over at him and smiled. "He told me he wasn't going to try and take my daddy's place, but that he'd be honored to be a dad to me if I'd let him."

Tears filled my eyes, and my heart felt like it was going to explode. "And what did you say?"

His eyes grew teary as she kissed his cheek. "I said yes, that I would love for him to be my dad."

Justin hugged her hard. "And I'll never forget those words for as long as I live."

Ellie stepped back, and Justin looked up at me. "I got a yes from one of my girls, but now I kneel here, waiting on an answer from the other." He kissed my hand, and held it tight. "I love you, Meghan. And I will love you until the end of time. I feel like I've waited a lifetime to find you. Now that I have, I'm not letting you go. With that being said, I have one question to ask you."

I held my breath, and my knees grew weak. I'd dreamed about the day I'd hear that question come out of his mouth.

He held up the ring. "Will you please be my wife?"

Tears flooded down my cheeks, and I fell to my knees. "Yes!" I cried. "I'll be your wife."

My fingers shook as he slipped on the ring, and then he kissed me. It was the best feeling in the world. Nothing existed except us, in that moment. I was going to hold onto that feeling for the rest of my life.

Ellie flung her arms around us, and we hugged her tight. "I can finally get what I've always wanted!" she shouted excitedly.

Brows furrowed, Justin and I looked at each other before turning to her. "What could you want that you don't already have?" I asked.

She giggled and let us go. "A baby brother or sister. You need to get married soon so I can have one." She grabbed the water pail and ran down to the water to get more.

Justin pulled me into his arms. "I'm good with that. What about you? We could get married this winter and get busy making those babies."

Leaning up on my toes, I wrapped my arms around his neck and kissed him. "Sounds good to me. The sooner I marry you, the happier I'll be."

He smiled, and cupped my cheek. "Couldn't agree with you more."

THE END

A NOTE FROM THE AUTHOR

Remember the message in the bottle when Justin and Meghan were on the private island? Be sure to check out LOVE AGAIN to find out the story behind it. If you're new to my books, I like to intermingle my characters, even if they're part of a different series. It's fun letting them appear in other stories.

ABOUT THE AUTHOR

New York Times and *USA Today* bestselling author L. P. Dover is a southern belle living in North Carolina with her husband and two beautiful girls. Before she began her literary journey she worked in periodontics, enjoying the wonderment of dental surgeries.

She loves to write, but she also loves to play golf, go on mountain hikes and white water rafting, and has a passion for singing. Her two youngest fans expect a concert each and every night before bedtime, usually Christmas carols.

Dover has written countless novels, including her Forever Fae series, the Second Chances series, the Gloves Off series, the Armed & Dangerous series, the Royal Shifters series, the Society X series, the Circle of Justice series, and her stand-alone novels *It Must've Been the Mistletoe* and *Love, Lies, and Deception.* Her favorite genre to read and write is romantic suspense, but if she got to choose a setting in which to live, it would be with her faeries in the Land of the Fae.

L.P. Dover is represented by Marisa Corvisiero of Corvisiero Literary Agency and Italia Gandolfo of Gandolfo Helin & Fountain Literary Management for dramatic rights.

For More Information:
www.lpdover.com

facebook.com/lpdover

twitter.com/LPDover

bookbub.com/authors/l-p-dover

Breakaway Series

Hard Stick

Blocked

Playmaker

Off the Ice

Forever Fae Series

Forever Fae

Betrayals of Spring

Summer of Frost

Reign of Ice

Second Chances Series: Love's Second Chance

Trusting You

Meant for Me

Fighting for Me

Intercepting Love

Catching Summer

Defending Hayden

Last Chance

Intended for Bristol

Gloves Off Series: A Fighter's Desire: Part One

A Fighter's Desire: Part Two

Tyler's Undoing

Ryley's Revenge

Winter Kiss: Ryley & Ashley [A Gloves Off Novella]

Paxton's Promise

Camden's Redemption

Kyle's Return

Armed & Dangerous Series: No Limit

Roped In

High-Sided

Hidden Betrayals (Coming Soon)

Circle Of Justice Series

Trigger

Target

Aim

In the Crossfire (Coming Soon)

Society X Series:

Dark Room

Viewing Room

Play Room

ROYAL SHIFTERS SERIES

Turn of the Moon

Resisting the Moon

Rise of the Moon (Coming Soon)

A Very Merry Christmas Series:

It Must've Been the Mistletoe

Standalone Titles

Love, Lies, and Deception

Anonymous

Going for the Hole

CHILDREN'S BOOKS –

MOONLIGHT AND ALEENA SERIES

Moonlight and Aleena: A Tale of Two Friends

Keep reading for a sneak peek at GOING FOR THE HOLE by L.P. Dover.

GOING *for the* HOLE

NEW YORK TIMES AND USA TODAY
BESTSELLING AUTHOR

L.P. DOVER

Chapter One—Lucas

"You sure this is a good idea?" My brother tossed me a shirt and I put it in my suitcase, along with a month's worth of clothes.

Sighing, I zipped up my luggage and ran a hand through my hair. Aiden stared at me, his brows furrowed in concern. He looked like our mother with his light blond hair and blue eyes. She'd be giving me the same expression, if she were alive today. Sadly, we'd lost her five years ago.

"Look, I know what I'm doing." I gestured toward the

door. Down the hall was a whole room filled with nothing but my trophies. "I've won too many tournaments to count. Hell, I could quit now and be set for life. But I need a break, before I burn out."

Aiden blew out a huff and threw his arms in the air. "All I'm saying is that you're on a roll right now. You're kicking ass in the tour."

He was right, I was. Competing in the PGA Tour had been the highlight of my life for the past nine years. No one had yet to beat my driving record. I had sponsors, a manager who happened to be my father, and a team of people who worked for me—including Aiden . . . my younger brother of five years, who also happened to be my well-paid caddy.

I picked up my suitcase and walked past him into the hallway. He followed me down the stairs to the front door, where his bags sat, packed up and ready to go. "Are you trying to say you *don't* want an all-expense paid trip to Myrtle Beach?" I asked.

A slow smile spread across his face. "I want the damn vacation, brother. Don't forget, I'm the pack mule who has to carry the clubs for your ass. You wouldn't make it one hole without me."

"Exactly." I burst out laughing, and his grin grew wider.

"I guess you know what's best." He looked serious once again. "And I want you to be smart about this. So, if you want to take a break, I'm all for it. Spending a month at the beach sounds pretty damn good to me. I just know our father's not going to like it."

My dad had a habit of being my manager first, father second, even though his intentions were good. He'd spent his life on the golf course, earning a name for himself. After my mother died, he passed his clubs down to me, along with his legacy. Aiden enjoyed the sport, but his talent laid with the calculations. He knew exactly what club to give me for each shot, and he was always spot on.

A car door slammed outside, and I opened the front door.

Noah Bradfield, my best friend since elementary school, lifted his arms in the air with the biggest smile on his face. "You ready, cocksuckers?"

Personal trainer by day, he was known by the media as my bodyguard—mostly because he was always around. I didn't need one though, as I was more than capable of taking care of myself. But he liked the attention, and it broadened his business. Besides, the ladies loved him, and he was fun to have around.

"Hell yeah," I shouted, tossing him one of my smaller bags. "Since I'm paying, you can load up the car."

Groaning, he carried my bag to the shiny, black Cadillac Escalade and tossed it inside.

"Dad's not going to like this," I agreed, turning to Aiden, "but he'll have to get the hell over it. I've given up nine years of my life. It's about time I have some fun." Granted, I belonged on a golf course. Out there, I felt at peace. Competing was a different story though. It could be stressful, wearing me down hole by hole. And lately, the pressure had become too much, especially with all the new blood joining the tournament each year.

Aiden reached down and picked up one of his suitcases. "Let's put our worries behind us and go have some fun. I'm not going to ruin it for you."

I patted him on the back. "Thanks, bud. I'd appreciate that."

He picked up his other suitcase and loaded it in the back of my car. Noah rushed up the front stairs and rubbed his hands together. "So . . . what's on the agenda tonight? I say we go to some strip clubs, cruise the strip, and get laid."

Chuckling, I laid my arm over his shoulders. "Sounds like a plan."

Chapter Two—Ashley

"You should start feeling better tomorrow." I ruffled Jacob's chestnut-colored hair and he smiled up at me through his tears. His dimples made my heart melt. The poor thing had strep throat, and I'd just given him a penicillin shot. They hurt like hell, but it was the fastest ticket to feeling better.

Jacob's mother lifted him in her arms. "Thank you, Dr. Locke. I know it's after hours."

I waved her off. "It's quite all right. Give us a call if he gets worse."

She nodded. "I will. We're just going to go home, eat some Popsicles, and watch movies."

Jacob's face lit up and he hugged her tight. "Yay, no homework!"

My nurse, Britney, escorted them down the hall with her angelic smile and bright pink scrubs. She had an effortless way with kids, which was the reason I'd hired her to be my assistant.

As I headed toward my office, I unbuttoned my lab coat. Normally, I'd be eager to get home by this point in the day, but today I didn't mind working late, since I had the next ten days off.

"Dr. Locke?"

I turned around and Karen at the front desk held up the phone. She was a close friend of my mothers, and a great receptionist. "Dr. Locke's on the phone."

"Which one?" I asked, chuckling. There were three of us, but technically only two now. My father had retired, leaving me and my older brother to run the practice.

Karen grinned. "It's your brother."

"I'll take it in my office." It was the phone call I'd been waiting on all day.

Soon, he'd be marrying a former NFL star's daughter who was a couple years younger than me and never worked a day in her life. She loved my brother more than anything—which was why I liked her—but the woman didn't know what it was like to live in the real world. And when she asked if I'd be her maid of honor, I couldn't say no. Unfortunately, being a bridesmaid meant I had to endure the bachelorette week. It couldn't be just a weekend for her; it had to be an entire week. Worse, I had no clue what she had planned.

Once in my office, I draped my lab coat over my chair and sat down. Line two flashed on my phone and I took a deep breath before picking it up. "Hey, Cam."

"Hey, sis. How was the office today?"

"Busy. If you weren't such a lazy ass, you could've helped me," I teased.

He burst out laughing. "It would have been a little difficult, considering I was out in the middle of the ocean all day."

"All right, rub it in. But in all honesty, it wasn't bad. You know I can handle this place on my own."

For his bachelor week, he decided to go deep sea fishing with his buddies before they all joined us the following week for the wedding. I could hear his friends laughing and carrying on in the background. "I know you can, Ash. Thanks for working late tonight." Cameron cleared his throat. "I guess you know why I'm calling. I figured you'd want to hear it from me first, before you speak to Olivia."

I bit back my groan and rested my head on the desk. "What am I in for this week?" Usually, my weekends consisted of healthy food and wine, not partying or going to strip clubs. However, I did have a feeling we were going to be visiting a club owned by Olivia's cousin, the guy who also happened to be one of my patients, and extremely good-looking. He'd been trying to get me to visit there for months.

Cameron cleared his throat. "Well, it's something that might interest you. I know you haven't done it in a couple of years."

There was only one thing that Olivia and I had in common . . .

"She wants to go golfing?" I asked, not really believing it. I used to be pretty good at it, but golfing was the last thing I expected her to want to do before her wedding. I figured she'd want to go away to a tropical island somewhere.

A laugh escaped his lips. "Yep. You're all staying at the Emerald Dunes Golf Resort. That way she can be there to handle any wedding stuff that might come up. She thought a few days of golf would help her relax. Not to mention, they have the best spa around. Play a round of golf each day, and then soak up in the spa. How does that sound?"

Not too bad, actually. Luckily, one of Olivia's three bridesmaids was a friend of mine, Harper Welch. The other two were her sorority sisters. Harper had been our neighbor and childhood friend growing up. We were inseparable, even when we'd all went away to college. "I'm sure I'll manage," I assured him. "I know Harper and I will have fun."

"I'm counting on it." I could hear the smile in his voice. "Tell Harper I said hello."

"Will do. We'll have to all get together for dinner once the wedding chaos subsides."

He chuckled again. "Definitely." A group of guys shouted in the background and he sighed. "I gotta go. Have fun."

"You too."

The line went silent, and my cell phone beeped inside my purse. There were two missed text messages. One from Harper, and the other from Olivia.

Harper: Looks like we're playing golf the whole week. I suck at it!

I texted her back. She didn't suck at it. Actually, she was pretty good, or at least, she had been when we last played a couple of years ago.

Me: You'll do fine. It's been just as long since I played, so we can be bad together. 😊

Harper: Kill me now. I'll meet you at the resort. Say around 9 tonight?

Me: See you then!

I closed out and read the one from Olivia next.

Olivia: I've decided on a spa and golf WEEK! Hope you're ready for some fun. Call me!

Taking a deep breath, I called her back, trying my best to get into the bachelorette frame of mine.

"Hey girl," she greeted excitedly.

"Hey."

"You ready for a wild week at the beach? I know it's last minute, but you have a suite with your name on it."

Her enthusiasm made me smile. I did need an extended vacation away, so I was sure as hell going to make the best of it. "I can't wait."

Made in the USA
Monee, IL
24 March 2022